THE WORLD
IN HICKORY H

by

Ardath Mayhar

The Borgo Press
An Imprint of Wildside Press

MMVII

Printed in the United States of America

SECOND EDITION

CONTENTS

FOREWORD

This novel was written in the 1980s, when the Cold War was a constant threat to everyone. While others created horrific scenarios, I wondered how normal country people like my husband and me would handle the situation, given the opportunity. This book is set in a location much like that of our small farm. The alternative lifestyle described reflects, in many ways, that which Joe and I lived or wished we could live. A few critics derided the notion of villains like the Ungers—but I have had old ladies from tiny hamlets in the woods ask me which of the families they knew were the ones on which I modeled the Ungers. In this neck of the woods, you can find almost any sort of person imaginable.

I am thankful that the blowup did not happen. Yet I think this human-oriented outcome could have occurred, instead of the power struggles some imagined; and I believe that people who think before they shoot are more likely to prevail than most. I also believe that the Draconian measures my characters had to take at the end of the book are preferable to living in constant fear.

—Ardath Mayhar
Chireno, Texas
August 2006

CHAPTER ONE

The owls were mourning when the lights went out. I'll always remember that, I guess, along with a lot of other things less appropriate.

Of course, we thought nothing of it at the time. When you've shucked off the rat race and gone completely back to the land the way Zack and the kids and I had done, you don't really pay that much attention. Mainly we enjoyed being able to read by good clear light, so we kept that skinny link with our old world, though it meandered down our rutted two-track road, across the hickory flat, up through Jansen's marshy pasture, and lord knows where before hitting the highway and civilization.

Actually, it stayed out about as much as it did on. Let a cloud as big as your hat come up, and the power would go...though I'll admit that it did stay on, by some miracle, the time a tornado ripped through and carried our calf shed across two fences into the hog pasture. Anyway, it didn't surprise us a bit when the floor lamp gave a little crackle, and we were left in the ruddy glow that came through the window in the wood heater. The children always loved getting out the big oil lamps and trimming the wicks, then sitting around swapping tales in the mellow light.

We sat there that night, snug and close and as happy as it's ever given to people to be, and never once did we suspect that the world had just come to a big, fat, blazing end. A batch of hickory nut fudge was in the middle of the table, and Zack was whittling shutter pins from a sapling we had to take out of the new garden ground. I was making willow-switch baskets, and the two youngsters were halfway playing Monopoly and halfway keeping up conversation with us between disputes about who had bought Park Place.

It was the first really chilly night of fall. Those unsecured shutters were rattling their catches in the brisk wind, making Zack cut away faster than usual. Before Grandmam's old cuckoo clock got around to announcing nine o'clock, he had the whole pile done, and we made a procession to light his way so he could fit them into the hasps. Then we all stood in a close knot, Zack's arms around me, mine around Jim and Sukie, while they tried frantically to keep from setting the whole mess of us afire with their candles. For a long moment we were secure. Totally, unreservedly secure.

It hadn't always been so. For too many years, we had battled to make our way in the foaming insanity that was the modern world. We were farm folks, true, with family land back down here in Hickory Hollow, but nobody had been able to do more than barely exist in this neck of the woods since the Depression. Even the wars hadn't livened it up any. Young people had to go out—down to Houston or up to Dallas—to make a living.

Zack and I had grown up together, neighbors on two small, hard-run farms at the back of beyond. We'd seen our parents manage and scrimp and make do, and we'd felt ourselves to be too sensible to try that sort of life. So when we married we took ourselves down to Houston and both of us got pretty good jobs. We took night courses and managed to work into better-paying fields as time went on. Of course we acquired our note and house payments, as well as some hefty hospital bills when Jim came, then again with Sukie. Still and all, we'd been raised by folks who counted debt just a half step above sin, so we didn't have a lot of time payments. Anything we wanted, we waited for until we could pay cash.

And that got harder and harder. By the time Jim was four and Sukie two, Zack was running a fair-sized photo lab, and I was doing draughting for an architectural firm. Still, the money we tried faithfully to save every month stacked up terribly slowly, beat our brains as we would.

The day came, along about our tenth year in Houston, when we sat down to supper at the same time for the first time in a month and proceeded to have a slam-bang twister of a quarrel.

When the worst of the sparks had fizzed off, we looked at each other. Really looked for the first time in a long time.

Zack looked weary enough to die. He was bleached-out from his sunless existence, and even his vigorous brown curls seemed to have lost their zest. The big brown boy I had married hadn't looked so washed-out since he returned from Vietnam.

I knew I looked as bad. That morning I had avoided the mirror as I brushed my hair, for the ill-tempered lines that were appearing beside my eyes and mouth didn't suit my style of looks. I had always been a calm, quiet person, which Zack had claimed was deceptive packaging, for I'm as red-headed as they come. Now I felt as if I were a volcano on the verge of exploding.

Jim and Sukie were sitting there, scared and big-eyed, wondering what had happened to their parents. So did I. So, evidently, did Zack, for he straightened up slowly and looked at me and the children.

Then he said, "I remember when we were two healthy, sun-tanned people who worked hard with their muscles, got tired enough to sleep like a couple of mummies, and went out and chopped wood when they felt irritable. I think, Lucinda, that we've made one great big mistake."

I didn't have to ask what. I knew. Hard as my folks worked all the time I was growing up, stubborn as they both were when they got angry with each other, they had never, as far as I knew, had the sort of stab-where-it-hurts kind of quarrel that Zack and I had just been guilty of.

We're no fools. Once we recognized the problem, we went about solving it as fast as we could. Both our fathers had died, along with my own mother. Only Mom Allie, Zack's mother, still lived up in East Texas, and she had moved to Nicholson, where she had a niece. The farms were sitting there, side by side, empty and waiting. Lord knows, nobody up there would have given anything for them, they were so remote, even from good roads.

Now we both knew farming the way you know it only if you grew up working on one. We were both good carpenters, plumbers, herdsmen, horticulturists, loggers, metalworkers, managers, mechanics...in short, typical farmers. What our dads couldn't afford to buy, they built with their hands, their ingenuity, and things they scrounged from dumps and junk-yards. We had absorbed their ability to look at problems and to solve them by the osmosis of living with it constantly.

Now while the sum we had saved was nothing, if you planned on buying new clothes and color TV and all the expensive gadgetry that gets shoved at you constantly, it was more than the total amounts both our families together ever had seen in any ten-year span of time. It was enough to pay the taxes on the combined places forever and two days. It was plenty to see us settled, the house we decided to live in repaired enough to keep the weather out, some livestock and seed bought, and a good bit left over for whatever came along.

It didn't happen in two weeks. We don't operate that way. We dug in, and with a clear-cut goal before us, we made the fur fly. We doubled up on car payments and got that note off fast.

Then we put the house up for sale, mostly furnished. The new junk that we had bought for it was made for city living, and we knew that the old houses that waited up there in the woods held enough of everything we'd need. Only the really valued things went with us—the dollhouse Zack had made for Sukie. The small splint-bottomed chair I had made for Jim's second Christmas. The bookcases we had built over the years to hold our incredible library.

By the time the house sold, we had done most of our moving, taking carloads of things, with a U-Haul behind, up and storing them in self-storage places. We had given notice a little early, so we would be free to clean the house properly before the new owners moved in. All four of us pitched in and dusted and mopped and vacuumed like mad, and all the time the children were singing at the tops of their voices, "We're goin' to live in the WOODS! We're goin' to live in the Woods!"

We left Houston without a backward glance, and we haven't been back in the four years since. The miles rolled away under our wheels, and we all took up the refrain... "We're goin' to live in the WOODS!"

Mom Allie was in seventh heaven. We had tried to get her to come down and live with us, but she, in her mature wisdom, had figured out Houston a long time before we ever did. "It'd be the death of me," she had said. As it was, she had the rear half of an odd little duplex, which gave her a huge back yard to marshal into blossom, fruit, and produce. We stayed with her for a night or two while Zack and I stocked up on tools and nails and roofing tar and window glass. Then we tried to get her to move out with us, back onto the farm.

Her gray eyes twinkled as she said, "You get things all nailed down and shined up. Then I'll see about it. I don't figure on getting roped into roofing and such, at my age." But she really meant, I'm sure, that we would need a while to get ourselves shaken down into this very different life, and an older person standing there to ask questions of would prevent us from using our own heads. She's a doll, Mom Allie.

Well, the house we chose was the one that Zack's great-granddad had built right down near the river in Hickory Hollow. It was originally build of logs, squared and notched and chinked with the mix of mud and straw they used to call "cats." Later generations had added rooms at the back and sheathed the whole thing in cypress planks, hard as iron.

The roof had lost most of its shingles, and the windows were more holes than glass, but it sat as solid and strong as a fort on its little rise that gave a bit of a view out over the Hollow. A deep-cut creek meandered around the east side of the garden spot and off toward the hidden river to the south. Then to northward the land rolled gently, climbing to the wooded ridge that broke the worst of the north wind in winter. Most of the hundred and twenty acres that were ours, mine from my folks and Zack's from his mother by deed of gift, were visible from the porch that wrapped itself around three sides of the house.

Jim and Sukie loved the place the first time we ever took them there on a long-ago visit to Mom Allie and Paw-Paw. Now they could hardly believe they were actually going to live there "for ever and ever and ever," as Sukie kept saying under her breath.

We moved in in June. That summer was a breathless

time of labor and fun and exhaustion and laughter and figuring-out and making-do. Before the November rains came, chill and gloomy, we had a good tin roof over our heads, aluminum windows fitted into the frames, the chimney rebuilt from base to top. Not to mention a whale of a garden planted, harvested, and canned in a huge pressure canner that had been my grandmother's.

Even the cold wet pony ride to school hadn't dampened the children's enthusiasm. Of course, the school district would have sent the bus out to the end of our lane, as the law required, but they would have spent the winter stuck in the mud. We figured that warm clothing, rain gear, and a pony would do quite nicely, and it did. The children were the envy of every other child in grade school.

The years since have been solid joy. We've put in our own power systems, little by little. A Savonius Rotor generates juice for the well pump. Homemade heat-grabbers siphon sun heat into the house all day. We were almost ready to connect up a series of rotors to provide our own reading light. So the lack of the commercial variety didn't really bother us a bit. Some dead tree or loose limb was always falling onto the line, and it took a long time for the power company to get out this far to fix it. We just didn't think about any more sinister reason for the outage.

Still and all, after ten days we were beginning to wonder. It was time for our monthly trip into Nicholson to get supplies of nails and coffee and what we called our vain unnecessaries, so we intended to report the trouble to T P & L while we were there.

I loaded our rattly old pickup (we'd traded the car for something useful) with canned stuff and shelled hickory nuts and quilt scraps for Mom Allie; then we climbed in and took off for the fifty-mile jaunt. It was a perfect November day, chill and damp and gloomy, as it had been ever since the night the lights went off. The low-hanging cloud seemed, once we got up into the higher ground, to be oddly colored, thicker, and somehow dirtier than I could ever remember seeing it.

It was a shame the children couldn't go, but they had both come down with the long-lasting sort of miserable colds—maybe flu—just in time to miss more than a week of school, and I wasn't about to let them get out into this weather. They were still looking dragged-out and pale, and I was hoping to get them in shape to go back to school by Monday.

We went bounding along our track, up to the dirt road that the county "maintained" in summer when the fishermen were going back down to the river with their boat trailers, then out onto the oiltop, some eight miles from home. You couldn't say that we were overrun with neighbors, but there were a couple of houses along the way, and I'd always waved at Mrs. Yunt and Grandpa Harkrider as we went by. Nobody seemed to be at home, though. No face appeared at a window as we clattered by, and even more strangely, Grandpa Harkrider's front door was swinging open to the wind.

We stopped, and I went up the path and closed it firmly, thinking that somehow this day was starting out to be one of those odd ones. It got stranger as we went along. Penrose was so small that if you hiccupped as you went through you'd miss it entirely, but there was always a car or two at Mrs. Benton's gas station-store and two old codgers sitting on an uprooted slab of concrete watching the weather and the cars on the highway.

Except today.

There wasn't a soul in sight in Penrose or Manville. Mrs. Benton was closed—and Mrs. Benton was never closed on Friday. Not even the day of Mr. Benton's funeral. The neat consolidated school halfway between the two hamlets should have been parked all around with cars and buses, and the long stretches of glass should have been lighted on this dark day. The parking lots were empty, the windows dark.

By now, we were feeling more than a little unsettled. I kept opening my mouth to say something about it, and Zack kept looking closely at every house we passed. Not one of them showed a sign of life. It was like some sort of dream, and I kept thinking that I'd wake up and really start the day. But the closer we got to Nicholson the more I realized that I was never going to start a day with the same feelings again.

Nicholson looked like the morning after a carnival.

Stuff was blowing around the streets in sodden drifts. Dogs were wandering around, lost and forlorn-looking. One house in maybe ten had the front door closed, and wary-looking faces would show for a minute at a window when we chugged by.

We lit a shuck for Mom Allie's. When we pulled around the drive and into her backyard kingdom, we saw with relief that her door was firmly closed, and a dim light was glowing inside her kitchen. She heard us coming, too, and the door flew open as soon as we pulled to a stop.

"Knew you'd be comin' in this week. Knew, too, that you never turn on Jim's little radio. Come in, come in, and let me tell you about the end of the world." She bustled us into her kitchen, where she had a coal-oil stove set up on top of her old steamer trunk, with a teakettle steaming away over one of the burners.

We took cups of hot tea into our numb hands and sat around the meager warmth of the burner, while she cut a piece of her Christmas fruitcake. I knew by that the news she had to tell was horrendous. Saving the fruitcake until Christmas week was ironbound ritual with Mom Allie.

While she settled herself and drew a deep breath, I held onto the teacup to keep from springing up and running out into the dismal day. My insides were squirming with dread, but I sat there and sipped the hot stuff and held myself down by main force.

CHAPTER TWO

Mom Allie took a scalding sip of tea, cleared her throat, and looked at us. Her gray eyes, usually so sharp and sparkling, were misted with unshed tears, and her hand jerked, clattering the cup against its pink-flowered saucer. She took several deep breaths before she found the courage to begin.

"You know—or, being you, maybe you don't know—that there was a real set-to in Korea last week?" We shook our heads. We'd given up, long before, on politics, international relations, and news. "Well, there was. We were sending notes to Russia, and they were protesting to the UN, and nobody knew what had really happened, even the ones who were there, I feel certain. Anyway, the President finally pulled up his socks and said straight out that any further encroachments into South Korea would mean war.

"They believed him, I guess. Or maybe some of our generals talked him into a 'preemptive strike'—neat way to get around saying an act of war, isn't it?—and the next thing anybody knew most of the East Coast, a lot of Colorado, a big chunk of the Middle West, and Houston went up in smoke. What else, I don't know. A few radio stations are still on, but they only broadcast twice a day, and what they say sounds like hindsight guesswork to me. Most of the reliable stuff comes from CB, or it did. Not many are still moving across country, now. Out of gas, most likely, and don't know how to get into the tanks at stations."

"But where did the people go who were here?" I interrupted. "We evidently haven't had serious fallout right around here, but who knows what might be in the next county? It seems ridiculous to me that anybody would pick up and leave a spot that's obviously comparatively safe and take off for the unknown!"

Mom Allie grunted, and Zack looked thoughtful. "The norther!" he said. "I'll guess that it carried the Houston and Gulf Coast fallout away from us. But what about the Colorado stuff? It's a long way off, true. Almost a thousand miles might do it, but with something that carries so high into the atmosphere, I wouldn't have thought so."

"The jet stream!" exclaimed Mom Allie. "There was a lot of comment on the weather news on TV about the jet stream looping down lower than usual. What if it was lying along a track, say, across North Texas? That just might catch up most of that contaminated crud and whisk it away to who knows where, mightn't it?"

It made some sense, at that. I've never found it in my heart to look too closely into the mouth of the gift horse that let us survive.

Mom Allie wasn't through, though. "You know, Luce, most folks just don't know how to live when the electricity goes off. All my neighbors ran around like chickens with their heads off. Kept saying that there just had to be someplace where everything was working normally. I will say those folks who spent all those years working with the poor little Civil Defense program did their best. Tried to make folks see that it was best to stay where they were and feel out the situation. Nobody listened, though.

"CD did get all the old folks out of the nursing homes and the little kids out of the Care Center and put them all together in the armory. They've got emergency generators there, and those kept some of the sick ones going for a while—the ones in respirators and such. But they've lost most of those who were going to go, now.

"Anyway, everybody who had a camp house or a farm lit out for there, which is sensible. The others just took off. Lord knows where they've ended up. But that's not any worry of ours."

She finished her tea in one long gulp and set aside the cup. "CD came by trying to get me to go with the rest of the incompetents. I told 'em I'd been livin' without conveniences all my life, up to the last few years. The lack of 'em wasn't going to kill me. Besides, I have enough fruit and vegetables canned and dried in this house to feed me almost forever."

I looked at Zack. He looked at his mother. "Now I suppose you'll come back to the boondocks with us, Mom?"

"Only thing to do," she grunted. "Can't warm this house—all electric. Got to go out in the shrubbery with a shovel, and in the weather we've been having that's no fun at all. All the water I have is what I caught in the bathtub, right off as soon as I realized what was happenin'. Farm's the only place to live like a thinking being, anyway."

Zack had been sitting there with his wheels going around. I could tell without even looking at him. So when he said, "What did they do with the old folks? You said, but I had other things on my mind," I was way ahead of him.

"Armory," his mother said, and her eyes began to sparkle. "Folks like Lucas Barnhart and Skinny Trotter and old Aunt Lantana Pinnery. All the brains and know-how in Nicholson are sittin' there in a corner waitin' for a chance to die decently and get out of the young folks' hair. A good six or eight of 'em who're still able and well, just older than their families were willin' to put up with."

"You still got that tarp you used to cover your root cellar with?" I blurted.

"And a good many old boards and pieces to make a frame with," she finished for me. Down went teacups, up came fannies from chairs. In less than an hour we had made a fair job of converting the bed of the pickup into a temporary camper, complete with Mom Allie's couch and chairs.

When we had that done, she went to one of her many cupboards and opened it. "How you fixed for winter?" she asked over her shoulder.

"If we ate all the time, we might get a tad tired of the same kind of thing, but we'd make the winter and part of next," I answered.

"Then I'll send all this stuff to the armory. They're feedin' those poor souls bought stuff."

I stifled a giggle, while we loaded the cases and cases of beans and corn and squash and jams and jellies into the truck. While I agreed, in principle, with Mom Allie's views on "bought stuff," I had lived on it for too long to believe implicitly that it was rank poison.

Then Zack went away to the armory, while Mom Allie and I went about salvaging what we could of her life. What could go onto the truck, we packed into small cartons, of which she always had a store, for she hated to waste them. The majority of the things, her lovely quilts and china and glassware and silver, we packed into the trunk and locked it, feeling rather silly as the locks clicked. When Zack came back, as he must, to scrounge tools and hardware, he could pick it up.

It took a while. Our stomachs told us it was about noon, when we were done, and Mom Allie turned up her coal-oil stove again, put on a huge pot, and began dumping every sort of vegetable you can think of into it. Before long, the smell began to make my inwards rumble with anticipation.

"Figure we'll need a good-sized lunch," she said, sitting down to wipe the steam from her glasses. Then she held the glasses up and said, "We'll need to go by the Goodwill and pick up a mess of these. Old folks need new ones just to see, pretty often."

Then it really hit me. If Jim and Sukie needed glasses, we'd just have to try our best to scrounge some. If they needed medicine, we'd have to make do on our carefully learned herbal remedies, for the stocks in the drugstores would be good for only a limited time. Dental work would go by the board, unless I could learn something about it. Zack was entirely too squeamish to mess around inside anybody's mouth.

Some of us were likely going to suffer—maybe die—for lack of the things we had taken for granted for so long. Well, people had survived for a long time without anything except their native wits, and I figured that we were well ahead of the game. We could find out what we needed, if not from our own thousands-of-volumes library, then from the nearby school libraries. Or from the one here in town.

I suppose my adrenals were taking up the slack, for I began to feel more vigorously ambitious than I had since our move from Houston. By the time Zack got back, I was pacing the floor with impatience to get started...with what, I don't quite know. Maybe survival.

The truck groaned around the curve of the drive, and Mom Allie beat me out to meet him. It was still mizzling rain, just above the freezing mark, but people started coming out of the pickup-camper. Old and young, dark-skinned and light. Lucas and Skinny, sure enough, their long thin faces so alike that they might have been brothers instead of cousins. Aunt Lantana, short and round, her dark-walnut face alight and interested. A young woman who was definitely Oriental—ah! Suzi Lambert, the Japanese student-bride Chuck had brought home from the University of Colorado. In her arms was a toddler with silken black hair.

Vera Nicholson, grande-dame of the town, descendant of the first family to settle here. Married her cousin so as not to lose the name, most thought. She hopped out next and shook her skirt down to a decent level. She held by the hand her little great-grandson, Sam Volpe. Behind her came two elderly gentlemen who were total strangers to me, though Mom Allie went up and hugged them both.

That seemed to be all, though I peeped into the truck to see if anybody had been stifled in the crush. Except for the cases of canned goods it was empty.

Zack looked over my shoulder. "I decided that all these extra mouths might run us short. I held onto this. They had canned stuff all over the place down there. A lot of the folks had left, and the ones who were still there seemed pretty numb, except for this bunch. They were just aching for a way to get out and do something."

"We'll fix up the other house, Dad's place, for some of them...the ones who won't fit into ours," I said. "Our systems can handle a lot more than we've ever burdened them with, too. We may have to do a good bit of hunting and fishing, this winter, though. Nine extra is a lot."

By this time, Mom Allie had hustled the newcomers into her kitchen and was doling out soup in any container that came to hand—teacups, small saucepans, bowls, mugs, tin cans, you name it. The soup was disappearing at unbelievable speed.

Miss Vera set down her cup with a sigh. "Alice, that's the first real food I've tasted in over a week. They swooped down on the nursing home and grabbed us up and off to the armory. Fed us on dried army rations for two days, then on cold canned stuff. I'd made up my mind to die, but Sam's folks had gone to Dallas for a week and left him with his nurse. Lord only knows what's happened to those poor children, but I walked over to the house, soon as I knew what had happened. Good thing, too. That fool woman was gabbling and babbling and getting ready to leave that child all by himself while she went off looking for her boyfriend.

"I sent her packing, took him in tow, and we were waiting out whatever is going to happen when Zack came in and offered us a chance. I may be stiff and cranky, by heaven, but I'm not useless yet."

"Well, now you'll get a chance to do some real bossin'," chuckled Mom Allie. "Never saw a woman in my life could get coattails to poppin' in the wind as fast as you can, Vera. We'll need you. You can see what's to be done and who's best to do it while the rest of us are still wonderin' what we ought to be wonderin' about."

The two old friends went off into quiet laughter, and the faces about them took on a bit of their cheer. Mom Allie had seasoned that soup with hope, more than anything else, and we all were warmed and strengthened by it.

We got the rest of the stuff loaded into the pickup in jig time. Most of our rescued crew had little but what they stood up in, so we dug out one of the "everything boxes" that Mom Allie kept for hand-me-downs from many sources and in all sizes. Moth-eaten jackets, sturdy army blankets, sweaters and scarves and boots and all sorts of useful things emerged. We bundled the whole thing up and tied it to the top of the pickup cab, wrapped in garbage bags to keep out the wet.

When we were loaded up, we looked like *The Grapes of Wrath* plus two. The pickup bulged fore and aft, above and below, with bundles and boxes. If there had been another vehicle (containing gas) to be had, we'd have commandeered it, but the flight from Nicholson to wherever had been nearly total, it seemed.

We crept along, the worn-out shocks letting the truck sag and sway as we rounded corners. As we rounded the last bend before hitting the state highway, we were brought up short by a stout figure in wrinkled khaki. It leaped into the center of the street and waved both arms commandingly.

"Stop that truck and get out!" came a bellow, surprisingly loud from such an unimposing man.

Zack obligingly stopped the truck, but none of us had the slightest intention of getting out of it. The round face, cross-barred by an ash-colored moustache, grew alarmingly red, and the person...official?...deputy?...whatever...tugged at the snap of the holster at his hip and stalked over, pistol in hand.

"You the one kidnapped them old folks from the armory?" he demanded, poking his red face toward the crack of window that Zack had opened. "You're under arrest, and you've got to get 'em right back where they belong, under U.S. Government auspices!" He exhaled the last word with such prideful emphasis that we were devoutly grateful the window was all but closed.

Zack sighed and leaned his elbows on the steering wheel. "These people are every one of them here because they want to be," he said quietly. "I'm not going to take them back to the armory to die with the rest of those numbskulls. Now you can shoot me—shoot us all—but you can't make us go back there."

"As for U.S. Government auspices," crackled a voice twice as commanding as any I'd ever heard, "I've had enough of those over the last sixty years to make me glad this mess has finally blown up in their faces. The precious U.S. Government has been made up of nitwits, timeservers, and busybodies for half my life, and they dug us deeper and deeper into debt and chaos with every year that went by. I'm glad it's blown to smithereens, Amos Ledbetter! Now you'd better get out of our way, unless you intend to add murder to stupidity!" Miss Vera Nicholson planted her short square feet on the wet pavement, crossed her arms on her sagging bosom, and glared at the bemused Amos with both thunder and lightning in her eyes.

"But Miss Vera," he pleaded, "my orders is to keep all the old folks in the armory. And to keep out-of-town looters"—here he glared at Zack and the loaded pickup—"out. I'm just doin' what I was told."

"You poor ninny," Miss Vera crackled. "You haven't seen anybody capable of giving an order in over a week. They're all gone, and they've taken most of the foodstuff out of all the stores with 'em. They left enough there at the armory for a few weeks, maybe, then they took off. You'd better scrounge up some way of living for yourself and let the rest of us go about surviving." She turned her back, and unseen hands hauled her back into the crowded truck bed.

Zack smiled sympathetically at Ledbetter and eased the truck into gear. "I'll be coming back to town for the rest of my mother's stuff, he said. "Don't think I'm a looter and shoot me." And he pulled away, leaving the damp, khaki-clad shape to dwindle in the distance.

The day hadn't improved a bit. The mist seemed to be on the verge of freezing on the windshield as we retraced our way, still looking for some sign that people still lived in the countryside. When we topped the long rise west of the Nagache Creek, and the long sweep of bottomland spread itself before us in shades of gray, we could see, away off to the left, a spiral thread of smoke.

Mom Allie gave a satisfied sort of grunt. "Cindy Howard got her whole crew over there into the woods at the Pioneer House," she said. "Maybe now they'll realize that she's worth more than a pot full of Ph.D.'s. That gal moved 'em right out of that all-electric brick veneer monstrosity they built, and put 'em right back in the tight old log house they grew up in. They'll live to bless a fireplace with cranes and that artesian well that flows out of solid rock."

"But how do you know?" I asked her.

She snorted. "What I'd do myself, given a bunch of slack-twisted gumps like hers. Lucky I've got a couple of kids with something under their hats besides hair."

She settled back. Her face, which had been so grayed with sadness and worry, seemed to be smoothing and brightening. "You know, it's not going to be near as bad as a lot of folks might think. We're going to be so busy we won't have time to get depressed and so tired we'll just purely have to sleep when we hit the bed. It's not going to be any cakewalk, but I think we're going to get stronger, smarter, tougher...or else we're going to die, every man jack of us."

CHAPTER THREE

That was the most concentratedly hectic afternoon I've ever spent. Our house, with the best will in the world, just couldn't hold nine extra people, plus Mom Allie. Two downstairs bedrooms, with the sleeping loft for the children, would have been wall-to-wall people. My Dad's house, though we had fixed the windows with tight shutters and mended the roof, was cold through, with no supply of wood to hand to feed the fireplace and cook-stove. That could be remedied with little trouble, but not in time for this night. Then I had a bright idea.

As we jounced along the last few miles, I suddenly gasped and caught Zack's arm. "Mrs. Yunt! If she's home, she'll be tickled pink to have some of these people with her, and if she's gone, she won't mind a bit. She's got bottled gas, as well as that good wood stove she cooks on when she's in the mood. And we hauled her two cords of wood up there, ourselves, when we cleared the new garden ground. There's plenty of food right here in the truck, so if she took most of hers with her, that's all right, too. They can stay the night there, all or part of them, and then tomorrow we can get to work fixing up Dad's place for them."

"See what I mean?" murmured Mom Allie. "Brains to burn, that one."

There was nobody at Grandpa Harkrider's, still, and no smoke curled from his stovepipe. As we went by I peered around the house and saw that his '71 Valiant was gone from the shed. Wherever he and his son had gone, I wished them well, though I questioned their judgment in leaving the river for the uncertain pickings elsewhere.

Then I looked down the road again, watching the ditches, now well filled with water, slide by in a splatter of mud. That slush, which had seemed so normal and winterish when we came, was suddenly suspect, now that I knew what had happened. What contaminants were falling all over our land, our river, and our woods right now? Without a Geiger counter there wasn't any way to know, so I shut it out of my mind and tried to exist, for this little time left, without thinking.

Too soon, we arrived at the oak-arched turnoff to Mrs. Yunt's drive. The door of her mailbox hung open like a dropped jaw, and already there was a litter of dead leaves and oddments collecting in its empty recess. No more mail. For a long time. Maybe forever. The thought was cold and lonely, and I mentally said good-bye to the few far-scattered friends with whom I corresponded on an infrequent basis.

I wondered, as we bumped gently around to the back door, why we hadn't thought it odd that our own box had remained so stubbornly empty, here in November when bright little catalogs seem to sprout in the box like fungus. The few times Zack or I had thought to check it, we had been unconcerned that even the meager light bill hadn't come.

Well, if nothing else, it was the end of bills, junk mail, and government forms. That alone was worth a lot. Mrs. Yunt had carefully locked her house and left a note for us under the clip on the screen door.

"Must go see about Julie," it said. "Know you'll come out in a while and check on me, so I'm asking you to take care of the place until I get back. Key's in the usual spot." It was dated October 28, which meant that poor Mrs. Yunt was probably in Houston when the bombs fell, for her daughter had lived there. She had been the best sort of neighbor, not much on visiting back and forth, but ready to lend a hand when she was needed and not too proud to accept help when she had her own difficulties.

However, we said nothing to our guests, just fished the key out of the well on its all but invisible fishing line and opened the house. We lit the gas heater in the living room to drive off the chill and the damp. Then Mom Allie and Miss Vera supervised the unloading of some of the canned stuff while Zack and I brought in armloads of wood and put it on the porch to dry.

When the wood-fired cook-stove was well alight, the fire muttering away like a purring cat, the kitchen began to warm up, too. Miss Vera set about making supper for the nine refugees, who had decided to stick together, at least for that night. There was a quilt box full of handmade covers and a closet full of blankets. Three double beds in two big bedrooms were made up, together with the twin couches in the living room. Then Zack, Mom Allie, and I headed out for home, well pleased with our day's work.

The children were at the big window as we drove up. Their faces, pale from their long bout of sickness, brightened when they saw their grandmother, and they met us at the door in a rush of "What took you so long?" and "Is Gramma going to stay with us always?"

We avoided distressing details, as we unloaded the necessary part of the truck's cargo and stowed it away in the spare bedroom that we had set aside for Mom Allie, if and when she decided to come to us. The kids, though, picked up distress signals out of the air. Their antennae would put radar to shame. They knew that we were unhappy about something, and I knew they knew. But I had had all I could take for one day. The world would have to end for them tomorrow. I simply could not tell them now, and I knew that Zack and Mom Allie felt the same.

Jim and Sukie are fine children. They still didn't feel well, but they had potatoes boiling for supper, the cold chicken from yesterday stripped off the bones and simmering in browned gravy, and a jar of corn ready to be frittered in the black iron skillet. That's another thing we held against the world we'd turned our backs on. It carefully trained its young to be incompetents—or worse. In the four years we had lived on the farm, our now eight- and ten-year-olds had grown into far more effective people than most of their teachers.

That was a strange supper. I kept trying to realize that the world had ended, but for us it hadn't even changed to any marked degree. The things we had brought back from town on our monthly trips had been, literally, unnecessary luxuries. I could find it in my heart to regret only smooth, effortless toilet paper. Even the electricity had been expendable, for Zack and I had studied our *Mother Earth News* for years, and had adapted many of their scrounged-part, homemade methods for generating heat and electricity to our own needs. We distilled our own fuel alcohol, built pedal-powered tools. Our systems, as they were, could give us much of what we needed. With a bit of work they could supply far more energy than we were presently in the market for.

Now I looked around the table at my family. Together. Secure, for this single moment in time. A part of me that had half wakened when we moved away from the city was now coming fully alert. An excitement was building, down deep, exulting at the opportunity to exert itself to the fullest. What greater satisfaction could there be than that of supplying the wants and needs of those you loved by your own efforts, energies, and skills?

As if he were reading my mind, Zack reached under the table and took my hand. His fingers were warm and steady, and a surge of hope pulsed through me. Given just a bit of good luck—winds that carried the debris of radiation away instead of toward us and rains that were reasonably free of contamination—we would survive. Both of us knew it with a knowledge that was ninety percent hope.

The wind died in the night. The misting rain stopped. We woke to white frost and a sky that was filled with a high haze. In normal times it would have been clear and dazzlingly blue, but now it was a pale gray. The sun was a paler blotch on the horizon. Dust-colored light filtered down the sky, looking almost normal, though dingy for such a frost-bright day. Ordinarily, the edges of the sky would be shades of shell pink, shading to lavender, while the sun rose in scrubbed clarity. Still, we couldn't quarrel with what we had. The sun did rise for us. For bow many millions over the earth did it never rise again?

I shook off that thought quickly and went about getting things ready for this first (for us) day after Armageddon. The children must be told, I knew, and I waited for them to descend their steep ladder-stair from the loft bedroom.

When the first pair of slippered feet appeared, my insides seemed to squeeze together with dread. Zack's grip on my hand was so tight that I knew he felt the same. We managed to smile, though, as Sukie jumped the last three steps, landing on top of Jim, who went down in a storm of giggles and squirmings.

If it had been a normal weekday morning, instead of the Saturday after the end of the world, I would have said, "Aha! You're well enough to go to school." And they would have given mock groans and halfhearted protests. Then they would have gulped their oatmeal, grabbed their books, and made ready for the long pony ride. But I said nothing, and something in my expression caused the two grins to fade, as they stood looking at me.

"Something has happened," Zack said, his nervousness making him abrupt. "It's pretty unbelievable...and it's very terrible." Here he stopped and looked to me for help.

I took up the burden, though my voice wasn't very reliable. "When we went to town yesterday, there wasn't anybody there. Not to mention. We hurried to Mom Allie's, and she had stayed, waiting for us to come. She told us...she told us that last week—remember the night the lights went out?—last week they dropped the bombs. All over this country. Likely all over Russia, too. Maybe all over the world. The radio isn't saying anything much, she says. But it means that everything has changed."

When I paused to collect my thoughts, Sukie looked at Jim. Then she said in a small voice, "No more school?"

"Not the school you've been having," I said. "There will be school, every day, for a few hours, but it will be here, and you won't have anybody but Vera Nicholson's grandson Sam and, in a while, Candy Lambert. Of course, if there's anybody around close who hasn't left and has grandchildren or somebody staying with them, they'll be welcome to come, too. We won't know for a while just who has stayed around and who has gone."

"Why did they go, Mama?" asked Jim, his gray eyes puzzled. "If we haven't even known anything was wrong, then this must be the best place there is to be safe. Why would anybody leave?"

"No way to know," I said. "Unless they're like Mrs.

Yunt, who happened to have to go tend to family business at just the wrong time. Or maybe they had family near Houston or Dallas or even farther off, and they felt like they just had to go and see if they were still alive and needed help. We'll never know, unless some of them come back and tell us."

"Can we listen to the radio?" he asked, though he knew that his little battery radio was his to do with as he pleased.

I nodded. "Just remember that the batteries we have won't last too long, and the ones in the stores, if any are left, will go bad, too. Don't...get too attached to the idea of listening. And don't expect to hear something all the time. Your Gramma will tell you what times there's something to hear."

They pounded away to bang on Mom Allie's door, and Zack and I sighed with a combination of relief and letdown. Children are always so much better equipped to handle major upheavals than adults. We keep forgetting that. As long as their own small unit is together and functioning, they seem to be cushioned against the traumas that attack us through worry and conscience and our strange arrays of undeserved guilts.

Breakfast was ample. There was so much to do, to see to, to rearrange in our small world that I felt we would need full bellies, if nothing else, in order to cope with the stresses of the day.

It was too cold for the children to be out for long, so I set them to loading the wood sledge with split stove wood from the extra pile at the edge of the newly cleared ground. That would go to Dad's house for the use of our new—what were they?—family, I suppose they must be. Today being sunny, our own wood fires would be unnecessary, as our heat-grabbers would be sending warmed air into the house all day through the south windows, to which they slanted upward like slides for midgets. That meant the children wouldn't be required to check the fireplace heater for fuel. I indicated sternly that the sledge should be fully loaded by the time we got back with the newcomers, unless one or both of them became certifiably shaky.

"No goofing off," Sukie hummed under her breath.

"Exactly."

"Now...now it doesn't seem like any fun to goof off,"

Jim said in an almost inaudible voice.

I knew what he meant. I felt myself that I should be working at peak capacity, making up, in some esoteric way, to those who were gone by my panting effort, as if that might ease their startled spirits in whatever dimension they might exist. I had an idea that all of us who had survived were feeling a bit of that compulsion to go out and prove our fitness for the lonely gift we had been given.

That went well with the amount of work there was to do, if our new "family" were to be comfortable in Dad's long-vacant house. Though they could have stayed on at Mrs. Yunt's indefinitely, that was a good three miles from Hickory Hollow. Too far for most of the older ones to walk in bad weather. And the pickup, though it could run on our home-distilled fuel alcohol, was a luxury we felt should be saved for foraging trips to town.

The three of us left the children hard at work and walked down the old path that ran up the creek, through the low-lying hickory wood that had first given the Hollow its name, out across a meadow that had been grown up to persimmon sprouts and sassafras, until we had brush-hogged it the past summer, getting it into shape to make hay for our small herd of Jerseys. We picked our way through the chilly stubble toward the low ridge beyond, where the huge old pecan trees marked the place where my own great-grandfather had built his home, after following his distant cousin from Tennessee to the Promised Land that was Texas.

There was still the stone he had painstakingly chiseled—HENRY HAZLITT, HIS PLACE, standing at the corner where garden met meadow. It made me stop, as I always had since I could read, feeling the realness that had been Henry Hazlitt, Aaron Hardeman, Zack's great-grandfather, and all the line of family that had culminated in the two of us. And now that was an eerie feeling, sure enough. Perhaps with us and our two youngsters that tough and tenacious line might come to an end.

I shook off the morbid thought and went forward to open the gate for Mom Allie. Then we both waited for Zack, who had stopped to check on Hazel, our youngest heifer, who was carrying her first calf. The pecans littered the ground, half lost in leaves and the berry vines that our best efforts hadn't been sufficient to keep out of the yard.

"They'll be out gathering these up first thing," Mom Allie grunted. "Your mother's grinder is still in the pantry—I saw it when I was cleaning up after her funeral. Even the ones without teeth can eat ground-up pecans. Give 'em a treat to change off on canned stuff."

Then Zack caught up with us, and we went into the house, opening the shutters and even the windows to let the cold freshness of the morning sweep the musty-old-house odors away.

Though mice had done a bit of nibbling, and dust was everywhere, we had kept the house in fair order, considering all the other work we had to do. I'd thought to keep it usable for one of the children, perhaps, when they grew up and had families. Now it took only vigorous sweeping and dusting, some judicious scrubbing, and then checking the flues for birds' nests and soot. Luckily, we had swabbed them down at the time when we were wondering which house to use, so after we had poked the old fish pole down the kitchen stovepipe to remove sparrows' nests it was ready for fires to be lit, as soon as there was wood.

The sunlight, stronger and brighter now, beamed through the windows in a flood, lighting my mother's reproduction Persian rugs to brilliance. The simple Grecian Revival couch and chairs spoke to me of home, parents, the endless safety of childhood, until I turned and walked outside, almost choked by the tumult of feelings that the past day had brought to the surface.

Chapter Four

It took a bit of adjusting to get the newcomers settled in. At first, drawn together, I would guess, by their traumatic stay in the armory, the nine thought that they'd stay all together in Dad's house. That was fine, but it was crowded. Then Miss Vera Nicholson realized that Sam, at six, was beginning to talk and walk and have the symptoms of his elderly companions. She got together with Suzi Lambert and they took us up on our offer to house any who wanted to come.

So it was that Suzi and her two-year-old Candy moved into Mom Allie's room, and Sam, to his great delight, went upstairs with Jim and Sukie. It was all her mother could do to keep Candy downstairs with her, for the black-eyed young one wanted desperately to be one of the "big kids."

This arrangement worked well, neither household being too crowded for comfort. Miss Vera, true to her steel-backboned traditions, stayed on to see that her old cronies kept their noses clean, and Suzi was kept busy and comforted by her task of keeping a supervisory eye on the children. Her husband's fate was, and likely would be, a mystery; yet, as he had been stationed in Colorado Springs, we felt his death to be almost a surety.

After three dazzling weeks that encompassed the end of November and the first week of December, the weather turned again. By now, we hoped, the worst of the radiation from the upper atmosphere would be cleared. (Our government's assurances that we used "clean" nuclear bombs had been heard with skepticism. Russia's, we felt, would likely be horrendous.) Only debris had been forced into the upper atmosphere. There was no way in which we could find if we were being slowly poisoned.

We were so busy, though, that we truly didn't spend any time in worrying about it. If we died, we would die working. If we lived, then everything we accomplished was that much to the good. So, while the clear weather lasted, Zack and Skinny, who had spent his life as a pulpwood logger, worked down in the big woods along the river, cutting firewood. Lucas and the two other men, Josh and Elmond Nolan, drove their frail bodies hard, splitting stove wood, hauling and stacking fire logs. And they all seemed as happy and healthy as boys, taking turns with mallet and wedges, loading the sledge behind Maud, our mule, calling and laughing as they went by our house on the way to add another stack of comfort to the burgeoning pile at Hazlitt's Heaven, as they had christened my old home.

It kept the older women busy mending ripped jackets and torn gloves and ragged knees in britches. We were going through our store of extra clothing and scrap material in jig time, and we soon realized that among the crops that the men were so enthusiastically planning for the spring must be cotton. Where they were to find the seed, we didn't know, but we knew that we must resurrect the art of making cloth, though, thanks to our invaluable back issues of *Mother Earth News*, we wouldn't have to reinvent the spinning wheel and the loom.

Three times we ventured the long trip into Nicholson, agonizing over the amount of gasoline we used each time. Though the pickup would eventually have to be made to run on alcohol, we feared that its advanced age might make it choke on a drink so different.

There were some few people still there, though they were fewer and shyer each time. Where they lived and what they ate we never found out, for the grocery stores had been cleaned out before our first trip in. The hardware stores had been picked over, but few had seemed to realize the value of nuts and bolts, nails and cotter keys and hacksaw blades, the small things that make the difference between a slick fast job and a long slow one. Screen wire was one of the things we collected by the roll, for Zack remembered his grandmother's tales of the hell every summer of her girlhood had been in the pre-screening days when mosquitoes came and went as they would.

We poked and pried into old storerooms and found remnants of obsolete stock—plow tools, harnesses and parts for them, clevises and pulleys for well ropes, and all sorts of things that a machine-oriented life had found no need for. They were worth more than gold to us. We appropriated one of the U-Haul trailers from the lonely Gulf station and loaded it up with long-term necessaries every time we made the journey. But there were other things.

We cleared the paperback book and magazine racks of all the stores that had them. I picked up this typewriter and boxes of ribbon and ream after ream of paper, and pencils and pens and notebooks and every sort of textbook we could find anywhere. Dyes and thread and needles and extra bobbins and parts for my very old treadle sewing machine. Aspirin from the drugstore, where the large generic bottles had sat undisturbed by other lookers, protected by the forbidding "acetylsalicylic acid" on the labels.

But so many of the things we needed had been either taken for use, which was as it should be, or they had been torn and burned and destroyed, as if some of our fellows had taken out their terror and insecurity on anything that came to hand. And, strangely, we found that the doctors, as they left (whatever their reasons), had taken with them their most used and valuable medical books. Perhaps they had gone or been called to places where there had been survivors...on the edges of the devastated areas. Whatever the case, none of them left family behind, and not one has ever come back.

It is difficult, from our unusual situation, to speculate upon the fates of those who left this area. When we arrived on the scene they were, by and large, already gone. Mom Allie had not been able to make any useful sense of the fragmentary and garbled bits she had picked up on her battery radio. The celebrated emergency broadcast system had evidently been left high and dry, with nobody who knew what had truly happened or what to do about it. They had tried, but they were useless.

So we scavenged, now and again, creeping like mice in

an abandoned house about the town that had been a bustling college town of 30,000. As the winter went on, however, we found that there was no longer any need for these expeditions, and we abandoned them. Still, I thought with satisfaction, now and again, of my deed on the last trip in.

Nicholson had been blessed with a really first-class library. It had an excellent variety of books, well arranged. It had art prints for lending, along with records and tapes. Its building had been built, in the early twenties, for a post office, and the construction was solid and likely to stay that way. When I had thought of it, I had gone through and taken what I felt would be most valuable to us. Then I had fastened all the windows securely, checked all the outside doors, and made a sign, which I taped inside the glass of the front door:

> The key is in the letterbox. Please use this library as you need it, but do close it tightly when you are through, so that the weather will not harm the books. This will be the way to the future for our children.

Maybe nobody would ever read the sign or use the place, but I felt better for it. Of course, the college had a fantastic library there on the park-like campus. It was one of those windowless monstrosities that they built at the height of air-conditioner worship, and it was inhabited by someone who spoke only through the barrel of a high-powered ride.

Though we tried to speak to him/her, there was never any answer, even to offers of help and food. Whether it was a fanatical custodian or a crazed librarian we will never know. Perhaps, even after all this time, that grim guardian still stands off nonexistent book pilferers. By the time the children need what is there, old age should have solved the problem.

(When we were sitting around the heater one night, wondering what the library guard ate, Sukie solemnly suggested that he/she likely subsisted on the offspring of the bats in his own belfry. Then we sat around debating whether that, in this case, might not be called cannibalism.)

Of course, there was much that needed to be done that

couldn't be tackled in the winter. Even with the small store of antibiotics that we had been able to winkle out of the drugstores' debris, we feared pneumonia. Without available doctors, hospitals, and stores of fresh penicillin, it would, we felt sure, revert to its old status of killer. So we didn't spend long hours in the cold and wet.

That left long winter days for talking and reading and writing. The talented among us took up whittling, and we soon had a store of bowls and spoons, hairpins and knitting needles, figures of man, beast, and what's-it.

Aunt Lantana often walked the damp way over to spend the day with us, and she proved to be a genius with a knife. I see that I've not described Lantana, and she well deserves description. She was, by her own calculations, somewhere approaching eighty. She was the color of warm copper, a result of her Indian admixture of blood. Tall and strong even yet, she had the dignity of a pagan queen. And she knew everything there was to know about the plants native to the area, plus a great deal about medicinal herbs that had been brought in by early settlers.

Under her direction, we gathered willow bark for tea (the original aspirin). We saved the husks from the black walnuts that we gathered from the woods for making dye later. We even garnered some of the big acorns, so that she could show us how to leach away their bitter taste and make meal from them.

"When you gets to my age," she said, "you can't tell for sho' how long you're goin' to be around. Now you need to know what I can teach you, and we'll do it just as if I won't be here another year."

So we went with her through the winter wood, learning to identify even the leafless bushes and trees, making lists of their uses. She showed us where the dry stalks of cattail rustled at the edges of the river shallows. "Every part of the cattail is good," she told us. "You can eat the root, boil the young 'tail' like sweet corn, catch the pollen for flour, eat the young green shoots. And make baskets from the fibrous green leaves."

Where we went with Aunt Lantana became magical, for she could see the nub that would grow into next year's poke sallet. She knew where the lamb's quarters would grow next summer. She could gather the resiny wads of sweetgum from a scarred tree and chew it up with stretchberries to make real bubblegum. All of us, young and old, went about with sticky teeth for days after that lesson.

Most of all, she showed us treasures around our own home that we had lived with unwittingly. A bed of comfrey grew in profusion between the horse lot and the garden fence.

We had meant to clear out "those weeds," but had fortunately been too busy. Now we had hot comfrey tea at bedtime, particularly when we felt as if a cold were coming on. And she laughed when we grieved to her that now we couldn't order any start of Jerusalem artichoke. We had a fencerow full of it that Zack's great-grandmother must have started and succeeding generations hadn't recognized.

All in all, Lantana came near to being the most valuable of us, for she showed us the thousands of edible, useful, helpful growing things that our culture had discarded as unsophisticated. And they worked.

So when her dark face was bent over her whittling, we listened to her tales and her advice, for we were trying to soak up all we could while we had her. And her tales were wonderful, all about great catfish that her father had caught from the river when she was a girl, expeditions to catch snakes to sell to "them perfessers" at the college, dark nights when hoot owls called and "de Boogeyman" lurked in the shadows on the way to the privy as they went with the lantern.

There were many of these dark days, for the winter was stormy past all recollection. Even at the risk of a wetting, we did much visiting back and forth, for all of us, I think, felt a need for other human beings. And on one such gloomy day, Lantana put aside her whittling and held her hands to her face.

"Law, Miss Luce, we've been lettin' our heads just set on our shoulders without workin'. You know what? Down this here river there's many a little old farm like this 'n. Now there's some folks on some of 'em, and that's all right, but on lots of 'em I feel like everybody's done gone off, just like

Mrs. Yunt and the old gentleman up the road. And every one of them has livestock!"

I looked at her in astonishment, amazed that we could have been so preoccupied that it hadn't occurred to us. "What was penned up is dead, by now, but there's got to be lots of cows and horses and mules and calves all over, fenced into big pastures, slowly starving to death for want of the hay in the barns that they can't get to. We've got to get out with the wagon and tools, Lantana, and see what we can do."

A break came two days later. The sun shone forth, weakly but with enough persistence that we felt the rains were over for a little while. Then Mom Allie, Lantana, Lucas, and I loaded hay hooks, wire cutters, pitchforks, and assorted halters and ropes onto the big wagon that Zack and I had built, hitched it behind Maud, and took off down the wagon track that followed the river for miles. I hadn't known that other farms could be reached by that route, but Lantana insisted that nobody had ever gone any other way in her youth.

"You can go 'way round by the road, twelve or fo'teen miles, and get there by car, but in the old days, we had to walk or ride a mule, and this was the short way. Go five miles along this old track, and you'll see ten or eleven little trails cuttin' into it. They goes to farms that's not more than a quarter mile from the water."

While we had no hope of covering the entire count of farms, we intended to go as far as we could and to do as much as possible in the space of a day. The first track we spotted some half mile from the point at which our own trail intersected the river track. We had to break out the axe, for saplings had grown up between the old wagon-wheel ruts. Lucas and I soon had them down enough for Maud to negotiate, and I ranged ahead, then, chopping out and laying by whatever blocked the way.

That first farm shook us. Penned closely in a new, tight barnyard had been ten weanling calves. They lay in a bunch, their skin hanging over their bones like spotted leather. The cold weather had kept them fairly well, but there wasn't enough flesh left on them to raise a stink.

We knew that nobody could be there, but I rapped on the

doorframe just the same, so deeply ingrained is the habit of knocking before entering someone else's home. The door flapped open in a gust of wind, and I jumped, but there was nothing alive in the house. And no vehicle was left in the garage. Whoever had lived here had gotten into the car or truck and gone away down the oil-topped county road.

"Why, why, why did they leave here where they had survived and could keep surviving, given a little luck, to go out into who knows what and take their chances?" I cried aloud. There was no answer then. There never has been. Not one of those who left has ever returned, and I suppose we'll never know what drove them out into the bombed chaos that was "out there."

We walked out into the pasture land, cutting fences wherever we found them.

"In the old days, this would have gotten us hung," laughed Lantana. "Used to be, if they caught you with wire cutters, they'd put you in jail."

Now, we opened the way to any surviving cattle to wander over wide reaches of country, and down to the river, where there was always browse. Then we took down the bars that closed off the big hay barn, so that they could reach the tons of baled hay that waited for them there.

When we felt that we had spent as much time as we could spare, we got back into the wagon and returned to the river, picking up my cut saplings all the way. We were learning to waste nothing, even whittling material.

CHAPTER FIVE

The river was high and brown with the runoff from the past weeks' rains. Most of the leaves had fallen and lay in yeasty drifts and piles, starred, still, with an occasional scarlet sweetgum leaf or golden spray of hickory. It was easy with the bushes bare to spot the next trail, which was well-used, beaten down to the bare earth.

We stopped, and Lucas got down to examine the tracks in the yellow-brown clay. "Pony track," he opined. "Cows, too, and calves. Sneaker tracks, big and little. Been used since the last hard rain."

Cheered at the prospect of finding another enclave, we turned up the lane. Even Maud seemed to sense welcome ahead, for she stepped out at a better than average pace. We emerged from the belt of woodland that lined the river bank onto a sloping meadow, through which the track curved upward toward a brown house that topped a low ridge. Smoke curled from a central chimney stack, and seldom have I seen so welcome a sight. Before we were halfway up the slope, we could see the figures of children pelting down the way to meet us.

The house sat in the midst of a young orchard, bare, now, but showing promise. A big garden divided the rear part of the orchard, and I could see great green collard plants, still heavy with leaves. The rest had been cleared and turned to catch the winter rain. Someone else was looking toward survival, you could tell by the condition of the land and the plants.

Three youngsters escorted us up to their home, chattering all the way. Carl was the oldest, a towheaded twelve-year-old with prominent ears and eyes that knew more than they intended to reveal. Carol, his just-smaller sister, must have been ten or eleven, blond and vivacious. The youngest, Cookie, was not more than four, as fair as her siblings, but tongue-tied at being among so many strangers.

They had been so cordial that we expected welcome from their parents. That, however, was not the case. They met us at the house-yard gate, which remained firmly closed. Their eyes were also closed—on the inside, which is hard to cope with.

"Curt Londown," the man greeted us. "Wife Cheri. We're doing fine, and we don't need a thing. Good of you to come by, but there's not a bit of good your wasting your time here."

Mom Allie can handle any situation ever conceived by God or man. She managed to engage the taciturn couple in conversation for a full five minutes. I said nothing, just used my eyes, and at the end of our very short visit, I knew that they were probably well-fixed for foodstuff, had plenty of fuel cut and stored dry, were preparing for crops in the spring, and were terribly afraid of something. Wariness fairly popped from the pores of both the adults.

I also discovered that Carl had met us with a small .32 pistol in his jacket pocket. As I looked down at him from the wagon seat, I could see its distinctive shape in the pocket of his jacket. As the other pocket bulged just as much, its weight hadn't called attention to itself. Who notices a boy's loaded-down pockets, anyway?

The discovery filled me with a foreboding that I hadn't known until now. What could have made a healthy, well-equipped young family so cautious—unless some danger was abroad, some immediate, here-and-now danger, unconnected with fallout and such?

As we turned the wagon and headed back the way we had come, I felt the weight of my own pistol lying against my thigh in my jacket pocket and was glad, now, that Zack had insisted that I bring it. And when we reached the river track again and turned to go farther along it, I got out and ranged ahead, as if I were merely stretching my legs.

The next lane had been used frequently, we could all

see, but was now drifted over with dead leaves and sweet-gum balls. I looked back at Mom Allie, and she looked at Lantana, who nodded.

"The Sweetbriers lives up here, if I don't misremember. Old folks, most as old as me. Their folks been on that place since heck was a pup. If they're there, they'll be mighty glad to see somebody, I know," she said.

Maud was, by now, weary of her new duty and ready to turn and go home. I took her by the cheek strap and led her into the track, and we meandered through yet another stretch of woodland. Around the first bend, we found our way sloping steeply to climb a sharp ridge that was lined with venerable hickory trees. Crossing over, we found ourselves in clean-floored pine woods...big woods, such as I had thought to be gone forever in the wake of the lumber companies and the pulpwood haulers.

Lantana looked up into the whispering roof far above us. "I see they never sold their timber stand," she mused. "They love these old trees. Went hungry, many's the time, but they wouldn't sell 'em. Down here, so far away from a road and so close to their house, nobody could get in to steal 'em. So here they be, still straight and tall and talkin' to the wind. And all the lumber companies and the pulpwood haulers and the paper mills are gone a-gallagin'."

We moved among the giant trees, even Maud's hoof beats muffled to quiet by the carpet of needles that lay thickly on the forest floor. Then we saw watery blue sky before us and came out into a narrow field that separated the pine wood from the garden fence of a small gray house that huddled among leafless chinaberry trees. There was no smoke.

Lucas pulled Maud up before the barbed-wire gate of the garden, and we all, moved by some strange instinct, went together into the heavily mulched rows, picking our way across to the yard gate. That stood open, and as we went through it, a small gray-brown form came trotting around the corner of the house bleating joyfully. It was a Nubian doe, and her narrow face was alight with greeting.

She nuzzled at our hands as we followed the sand path around the house to the back porch. It was a screened enclosure containing a washer and a chest-type deep freezer. The door was unlatched, and we found the door into the kitchen unlocked—violently unlocked. Something had torn the door away from its own locking mechanism, splintering the door facing as well.

I shivered, and Lantana laid her hand on my shoulder for a moment as I nerved myself to step inside. The kitchen had been ransacked. Cupboard doors had been left open, and broken glass, pots and pans, dishes, and loose flour lay in drifts across the bright linoleum. No sane person, scrounging for food, had done this. Pointless destruction had been the rule here.

Into the hush that followed our entry, there came a moan. That released us from our shock, and Lucas moved quickly into the next room through the swinging door at his right. A very old woman lay propped against a leg of the dining table. She had pulled the bright cotton tablecloth down and covered herself with it against the cold, but she was almost blue with chill, as well as with loss of blood.

Her short white hair was matted with dark clotting across the left side of her head, and the stroke that had split her scalp had closed her left eye with a purple swelling the size of a tennis ball. She had just enough consciousness left to know that someone had come and to let us know that she was there.

"See...to...Jess," she whispered as Lantana lifted her against her shoulder, comforting her as if she were a child.

Lucas took a knife from the kitchen, and I checked the load in my pistol. Then we moved into the living room, which adjoined the dining room. There was nobody there, so we went across it, down a short hall, and into a bedroom.

Jess was there. He had been beaten to death with his own walking cane.

The room was smeared and spattered with blood from wall to wall. Even the ceiling had dark brown drops across it in an arc, where the fouled cane had been swung high and down, scattering blood in its wake.

Lucas knelt beside the dead man and felt his cheek, flexed one of the hands. The gaunt old fellow was as calm as any doctor could have been as he rose and said, "He's been dead most two days. I've seen a lot of dead men, child. I was in the war. But she's been lyin' out there in the cold and losing blood for entirely too long. We've got to get her warm, then take her home with us. Nobody can stay here, even if it might be safe to. Somebody mighty ornery is in those woods."

"Now we know what the Londowns were so antsy about," I said. "They must have had a run-in with whoever did this...or could there be two batches of madmen running up and down the river or the road?"

"Unlikely," he said, turning back to the dining room. "Let's look on the bright side. Let's say there's only one crew of murderers loose around here."

In the short time we had been gone, Lantana had swept the worst of the debris out the kitchen door, and Mom Allie had lit a fire in the cook-stove, rescued a kettle from the battered utensils, and set it full of water from the rain barrel. The bottled gas burned blue under its copper bottom, and it looked unnatural to me after the four years I had spent using wood to cook with.

We brought a mattress from the second bedroom, which had been disordered but not destroyed as the other had been. With the blankets Lucas found in the quilt box beneath the kitchen windows, we made Mrs. Sweetbrier comfortable on the floor near the heater. As the iron grew warm, her color improved, and I blessed the big woodpile that had enabled Lantana to get a fire going in the potbellied heater so quickly.

A canister of tea had been heaved out the back door and lay, still tight-lidded, on the entry porch. We made tea in a fruit jar, strong and hot, and Lantana found enough sugar spilled on the counter to make it very sweet. With this warming brew inside her the old lady revived quickly.

One glance around her kitchen made her moan again, but she forgot the destruction when she looked up at me. "Jess?" she breathed.

I've seldom felt so rotten. "He didn't make it," I told her. "He's in the bedroom. In a little, we'll bury him, if you'll tell us where he'd have liked to be put. You'll come home with us, and we'll take care of you, if you'll go."

It wasn't soothing or comforting or even tactful, but at the moment it was all I could come up with. I kept thinking about our long ride back through the woods that would be getting dark in another two hours. I was in a hurry. She, more than anyone, could sense the reason for that.

"Yes. Of course," she said quietly. "I knew, really, that he was dead, or he would have come looking for me. He'd like to be by the garden gate, under the big chinaberry with the rose vine up it. Then we'll go. It's getting late, from the look of the sky."

It was a quick and simple funeral, the only one that I knew of during that entire death-filled time. Lucas, Mom Allie, and I took turns with a shovel from the garage, and though the grave we dug was shallow, we covered it over with heavy rocks from a pile by the fence, once Jess Sweetbrier was in it. Lantana knew the right words to say, and we all stood in the pale, late-afternoon sunlight as she spoke.

"Lord, You've seen fit to give the world a new start. We all know that that means hardship and suffering for us and for ours. Our friend Jess has been spared the tribulations that we must still face. Welcome him to heaven, Jesus, and guide our way as we go."

We found our patient lying still and pale, but she looked up as we came in and said, "Our car is in the garage. If they didn't ruin it, it should run...the battery was new last summer. We could go by the road and miss the woods entirely."

I looked at Mom Allie. She nodded. "You don't need to take a long, cold ride behind a mule, for sure," she said to Mrs. Sweetbrier. "I'll drive and Lantana can see to you. The three of us will go that way, and we will see what we can salvage of your clothes and covers.

"Luce," she turned to me, "Maud has to go back tonight. There's not so many mules left that we can risk one. Are you and Lucas game to take the wagon back?"

The thought of the thick woods along the river was now filled with dread. I knew that for my own self-respect I must go back that way.

The car, a 1980 Plymouth, started on the second try and ran like a top. The gas gauge sat on a half tank, which would give us more mobility than we had had with only the pickup for transport. Once we were sure that the three women would get safely away, we went back to the dreaming Maud, waked her with a cluck, and turned back toward the forest.

It was already dusky beneath the trees. Owls were hooting already, and as we turned into the track, heading home, a bobcat squalled in a thicket, to be answered by another up ahead. Maud picked up her ears, realized that she was headed, at last, in the right direction, and all but broke into a trot. We jounced along in the wagon, teeth rattling, but we were, if truth be told, glad enough to be moving at such a good clip. Neither Lucas nor I had any desire to meet those who had attacked the Sweetbriers.

The wagon rattled and squeaked, the harness chinked softly, but I kept my ears cocked for any sound that seemed alien or threatening. I was listening so hard that I almost missed seeing what was before my eyes. Another pair of eyes was staring into mine from the covert of a huckleberry thicket.

My hand came down on Lucas's shoulder in a thump, and he turned to look where I was staring. At that moment, three ragged figures rose from right, left, and ahead and Maud came to a halt.

They were women. Filthy, ragged, wild-haired, but definitely women. I kept my hands in my pockets as if I were cold, letting Lucas hail them.

"Evenin'." came his cool voice. "Might we help you ladies?"

The oldest, in the thicket at my right, stepped forward into the track, and I could see that she was wearing men's overalls, rubber boots, and a violently cerise sweater that emphasized her immense bosom. She was grinning, and I was not reassured by that awkwardly lipsticked grimace.

"Why likely you can, old man," she shrilled. "Me'n the girls just purely need a mule. Hadn't thought on it before, but seein' yours give us the notion, didn't it, girls?"

The other harridans, one very young, the other a well-used thirty, giggled but said nothing. Their pale gray eyes lent the only clean spots to their thoroughly begrimed faces, making a strangely sinister effect.

"Sorry," Lucas said. "We need the mule to help make

our spring crop. We just came down to check on the Sweetbriers, make sure they were all right."

The three cackled, high and shrill. "And were they all right?" yelled the woman to my right.

The three moved toward us before Lucas could answer. The younger two carried heavy sticks—they looked like hoe handles. I remembered Jess, and I yelled at Lucas, "Go!"

The old woman's hand whipped out, holding a knife, reaching for the mule's throat. I shot her through my jacket pocket, and she fell sidewise into a clump of sumac.

As Maud bolted, I got off one shot at the one ahead, but she dived into the brush. Then all I could do was hold on, for Maud intended to arrive home ten minutes ago, and the wagon just had to trail along the best way that it could.

I glanced back once, to see the two women bending over their fallen leader? Mother? Whatever. I shook with regret. I hated to leave even one of them alive.

CHAPTER SIX

We had come at an easy pace. The washed-out sections of the track, the holes interrupted by knots of tree roots, hadn't bothered us. Now they all but bounced us out of the wagon. And all that clatter and jounce was a drag on Maud, who soon slowed to a more reasonable gait.

When things had settled to a passable condition, I said to Lucas, "Do you suppose that was all of them?" My teeth were chattering so that I could hardly articulate; the growing cold and the realization that I had killed someone seemed to be trying to shake me apart.

Lucas turned his wise brown eyes on me. He held out his arm, and I leaned against him and felt him patting me on the shoulder as if I were Sukie's age.

"Child, be easy. There's more than what we saw, I feel certain. More than I like to consider on. But you took one of them out, maybe permanent. Only thing you could do. Had you not, we'd both be like poor old Jess Sweetbrier by now. Those critters weren't more than half human. I don't know who they are or what made 'em that way. Lantana will know. She knows every man jack in this end of the county, by reputation, if not in person. Just you be easy, now. We'll be home in another ten minutes."

The sun was down, the sky glowing with angry color when we pulled up between the big woodpiles into the backyard and Maud came to a panting halt. Zack was there waiting. He saw at once that something had happened, and his hands gripped me so hard they hurt, as he lifted me down.

"Mom said she had a feeling something was going to happen, after you left. If she hadn't had to get Nellie Sweetbrier back here, she'd have taken out after you. You should have seen her driving up with Lantana holding Mrs. S. and the goat standing in the back seat, looking out the window. In the days when there was traffic, there'd have been wrecks all along from folks trying to see what in thunder sort of passenger she was hauling."

He was babbling, something he never did except when under strain. I laid my head against his chest for a minute, then I looked up into his eyes.

"I killed an old woman, Zack," I said, holding my voice steady as I could. "She and two other women, younger, were waiting for us. They'd likely seen us as we came along and turned off to the Sweetbriers'. She started to cut Maud's throat, and I shot her dead. I think. I meant to. I believe I hit her in the throat.

"But the other two and likely more are out there in the woods down the river." And then my voice failed, and I felt tears creeping down my cheeks.

Lucas had quietly climbed down and turned Maud and the wagon over to Jim, who led her toward the shed. He told Zack exactly what had happened while I stood there, warmed by his arms, looking back down the tunnel of my memory at that red-sweatered form pitching into the sumac.

Then we went, together, into the warm house, where the lights, powered by their own Savonius and bank of batteries, burned defiance to the lightless world outside the shuttered windows. Inside the back door the shotgun was laid on a newly made rack. And I saw that the big mahogany box that had always held Zack's and my father's guns was open and empty.

"There's never enough death," I sighed, sitting down on the bench along the table and tugging at my cold, damp boots. "It's not enough to have the world blow itself to kingdom come. Now the mad rats are creeping out of the walls to kill off the rest of us."

Lantana came into the kitchen and sat on the bench beside me. "There's always been crazy folks," she said. "It'd be more luck than we deserve to have all of them be killed off. And, from what Lucas tells me, the ones you saw have been down here in the river bottom for a long time. The old woman—the one you shot—had to be the Unger."

I looked up, startled. Tales of the Unger and her brood had given two generations of children goose bumps around campfires. I could remember staring off over my dad's shoulder into the dark brush and thinking I saw secret shapes, moving, as he recounted the wild deeds of that mad harridan. Even his solid presence hadn't quite made up for the deep night of the woods round our fishing camp, the weird tremolo of a distant screech owl, the fluttering call of whippoorwills.

Lantana nodded solemnly. "Has to be. She'd be old. A big stout woman with a front on her heavy enough to shove down a wall. Scraggly hair, full of leaves and grass. And dirty. Dirtiest human I ever laid eyes on. My old Jake, fresh from the field in June, was sweet as a rose compared to her. You could smell her a mile before you could see her. And her chillun was the same; only time they touched water was when they fell in the river."

"But who was the father of her children?" I asked. I had always wondered vaguely why "the Unger" was always and ever a woman, with never a mention of a man.

"Who wasn't?" Lantana muttered. "I'll tell you, Miss Luce, anybody, old or young, black or white, who wanted to prove he wasn't scared of nothin' could do it by goin' off down there to her big old shed of a house and takin' her on. A good bunch of 'em did, over the years. She had chillun of every color you can think of. And some few of them that went never come back at all. Got so's nobody ever took more'n just enough to pay her for her...services. Safer that way.

"She had mostly girls. Or maybe she had boys, too, but she must of drowned 'em, because nobody ever knew of a one. Then the girls grew up—or grew up enough—and there was a whole new crew down there to tempt the money out of any man fool enough to go. It was a nest of bootleggers and whores fit to sicken a snake. Still is, I'd reckon!"

"Then there'd be more than just the two we saw with her," I said, slowly. "Maybe a lot more. Daughters and granddaughters. A whole crew of them."

"Way I figure it, they stayed down there for a while after

things came to a halt. Then they got bored, maybe, or wanted somethin' they ran out of, and went lookin' for people. No tellin' what's down the line from the Sweetbriers. There's at least four more families that have places frontin' on that road and backin' up to the river. Some may have stayed. Two out of three we looked at had."

I felt sick. "We'll have to go and see about them," I agreed. "Not knowing whether there's somebody else in the shape Mrs. Sweetbrier was in would drive us crazy. But we're going to be a lot more cautious around here, too. They'll get to us, eventually."

Zack nodded. "We're going to listen to the crows," he said. "And somebody in every group of us is going to be armed. I've told the kids already to make for the house the minute they hear the crows in the river woods talking about something moving. It's better to take cover from a fox or a wolf than not to take cover and have those hellions on top of us."

"We'd better go back by the road," Mom Allie interjected from the next room. "We can run that old Plymouth on some of your alcohol, if we need to. That way they can't ambush us in the woods."

I heaved a sigh of relief. The thought of going through those thick, secret thickets again, knowing that something irrational might be watching, had given me the shivers.

Lucas, rising and putting on his coat, said, "Time Lantana and I get on home. One thing, though. Tomorrow, first thing, let's send the kids to move the horses out of the low pasture. Those devils might kill 'em, just to be doing somethin'. And those horses are the future, don't ever forget it. The vehicles will run for a long time. We can make all the fuel we need. But parts are somethin' else again. And tires. Horses are the only long-term answer.

Zack nodded. "Smart thinking, Luke. We'll get them moved first of all in the morning. Then I figure some of us are going to want to go on and check out those other folks downriver. I'll not sleep much tonight, worrying about somebody needing us right now, that we don't know about."

We had adapted the old coal-oil lanterns that had been used when we were children so that they could burn alcohol.

Each of the old people lit one, and we watched them through the glass pane of the door as the two spots of clear light moved away and vanished in the trees. Then we went into the living roam to check on Nellie Sweetbrier.

She was lying on the couch, her head neatly bandaged, her eyes closed. When we hesitated, not wanting to wake her, she opened them and said, "I'm not asleep. Came sit down and let's talk a bit. Mrs. Hardeman is in her room making me a place to sleep. I was just lying here remembering Jess. We were together forty-three years. It'll take some getting used to, being without him."

"We'll keep you so busy that you won't be able to have time to grieve too much," Zack said, taking her blue-veined hand in his. "We are a going concern, here, Nellie. You'll fit right in."

"If we don't start dying of radiation sickness, or some plague that everybody thought was licked doesn't rise up again and take us off. Or those hellcats don't kill us all," she said bitterly. Her free hand twitched against the bright quilt that covered her. "I want you to tell me, right out, in full, what happened to Jess," she said to me. "I need to know. The things that I imagine are worse than anything that could possibly have happened for real. Tell me how he died, how he looked, how the room looked. It's only when I can see it like it really was that I'll be able to stop my mind from running around and around, making pictures of what might have been."

I looked into her eyes. There in the warmth of the wood fire that twinkled through the glass of the heater door, with the smell of stew filling the house with richness, with Zack's other hand in mine, the scene in that house downriver seemed already far-off and dreamlike. So it was that I could tell her, as if it were a story or a movie, exactly what Lucas and I had seen in that bloody bedroom where Jess had lain dead. I even told her about the trail of drops on the ceiling that had followed the arc of the stick that had beaten her husband to death. For I knew that she was right.

Only the truth, terrible as it was, would lay to rest her over-stimulated imagination.

When I was done, she closed her eyes for a moment,

breathing deeply. Then she opened them and said, "Thank you. That was bad, but he died fast. Must have gone out when they hit him in the head. After that, they weren't truly hurting him. And he didn't have to lie there and freeze and wonder if they'd come back to finish the job, like I did; all in all, he was lucky. Thank you, Lucinda."

Then Suzi brought a bowl of stew for Nellie. "Supper's on in the kitchen. The children are washing up, and Mrs. Allie is on her way."

So we left the old lady to eat her supper and to come to grips with her loss.

The long evening was before us, and we all congregated around the big heater. Our newcomer didn't seem to want to talk, but her face smoothed as our bantering and tale-telling accompanied the work of our hands. For, as it must have been in the long past, each of us was busy with some small but necessary task. The children were in a circle on the floor, a big bowl in the center, nutpicks in hand, as they picked out hickory nuts. A more tedious and frustrating job was never dreamed of, but when it was leavened with firelight and lamplight and stories of their grandmother's youth, it went almost effortlessly.

I had a lapful of socks, and Mom Allie and Suzi were mending knees in the children's outdoor clothes. Zack was oiling harness, rubbing the rich-smelling stuff into the dark old leather until it ran supple and living between his hands. No word passed between us of the discoveries the day had brought. The children knew what was necessary to make them cautious. We had no intention of making them afraid.

The bag of cracked nuts (Zack had shattered the tough hickories with his hammer on an iron block before turning them over to the children) went down at a slow but steady rate. Candy struggled with her fat fingers, being entirely too young to be trusted with a sharp nutpick. Eyes grew heavy. By the time the bag was empty, all four young ones were ready for bed.

When they had been bundled into their flannels and shooed upstairs, we turned to Nellie.

"Tomorrow we're going back to check on the other folks down your way," Zack said to her. "We'll take your car, if you don't mind, so we won't have to go through the woods.

"We need to know who is down there, if you'll tell us. "

She sighed, and her good eye closed for a moment. Then she hitched herself up and said, "All right. I hate to think what might be going on down there tonight. So."

She thought a minute. "By the road, you'll have a time knowing where to turn off to find the next house downriver from ours. There's what looks like a logging road, all arched over with trees. Thick brush on either hand. But you can tell, because there's a great big hickory tree just beside it. I mean a giant tree. Just past it, on the right, there's the track. The Fanchers live down there. Black folks, fairly young couple. They've got a bunch of children—seven or eight, maybe. The oldest might be eleven or so. Bill and Annie are good folks; just be careful how you approach them. They've had some bad experiences with white people. They came out of Tulsa...bought the old Barron place through a real estate agent.

"When Claude Barron found out his old family place went to black people, he nearly went crazy. Bad streak in that family—always was. He has sneaked down there and shot at them...yes sirree," she insisted, when we looked incredulous. "He tried to set fire to the house in the middle of the night. Just God's mercy that their dog woke them up so they could put it out before it did more than scorch their back stoop. Claude got them so nervous and suspicious that they hardly go anyplace or have anybody visit them.

"If they're there now, and I'd say they are, being sensible people, they're going to be antsy. Go easy. Blow the horn twice before you get to the house. They know the Plymouth's horn. When you get up to their back fence, stop and get out, all of you, so they can see you're not hiding anything. They shoot pretty quick, and I don't blame them."

She stopped for a moment, resting and thinking. Then she said, "About a mile down the road from their turnoff is a cattle guard between two old chinquapin trees. You can't see the house from the road, for the Jessups built their house way down as close to the river as they could find high ground. Just follow their road. It's on a dump through the low places, so it doesn't get underwater when the river rises. It may be that just Horace and Carrie will be there, or their kids may have come home, after the blowup. If they could. Two girls in college and a son in the insurance business in Shreveport.

"Next one is a big deal—brick pillars with a wrought-iron archway over the top. Greenwillow, they call the place. I doubt the Greens will be there, though. It was just their vacation home, even if it is the size of a small hotel. Anyway, I heard that they were spending the winter in Europe. If that's so, I doubt they'll ever get back, if they're still alive at all.

"Now you're almost to the end of the road. The oil-top ends at the edge of the Greens' property—they're the only reason the thing ever got oiled at all, actually. From there it's a muddy lane that ends in Sim Jackman's woods. Sim's there, I'll warrant. It's possible he doesn't even know anything at all has happened. He shuts himself in down there and drinks steadily through until the weather clears in the spring. He makes moonshine, too, but his is strictly for drinking.

"And that's all. I'm tired, Lucinda. Help me to bed, please." She closed her eyes, the purple lump an ugly splotch on her pale face.

When she was settled for the night, we sat about the fire. Zack, Mom Allie, Suzi, and I. We thought of tomorrow. I don't know about their feelings, but mine were filled with dread and a sick memory of Jess Sweetbrier's crushed head.

CHAPTER SEVEN

It was now the end of November. In the confusion, we had lost track of days, but as nearly as we could reckon, it was the thirtieth when we set out on our mission of rescue. It was one of those holly-berry days of dazzling sunlight and hard frost. We left the children spinning round and round in the yard, their bright jackets blurs of color. It was something cheerful to take with us on our journey.

And it was a journey, now. The violent weather of the fall had sent trees down across the road more than once, not to mention washouts and soft spots. Zack, ever practical, had brought his chain saw along, which sent us on fairly quickly. Mrs. Yunt's house looked as empty as it was as we crept by. Though we had secured things as well as we could, on the off chance of her return, it already looked desolate. And Grandpa Harkrider's place was a mess. One of his big old oaks had split at its fork and crushed his front porch.

"It's funny how quickly things go when there aren't any people around who care for them," I murmured, and Zack reached over and squeezed my hand, which almost sent us sliding quietly into the ditch.

We were alone. The consensus had been that we might have a full load of passengers when we returned. We, being a pretty tough combination, were the logical ones to go. We were loaded for bear, too. In addition to my pistol, we had the .410 and my dad's deer rifle, a very old Springfield 30.06.We didn't intend to fall victim to the Ungers.

It was a relief to reach the hard-surfaced, farm-to-market road. Even that, however, was littered with leaves and small branches and anonymous debris. Once, indeed, we had to edge around someone's shed roof, which had been blown over a fence and halfway across the pavement. The rest of the shed leaned awkwardly in the cow lot over the fence, its walls awry.

It was a long way around by the road, just as Lantana had said. Nearer twenty than the fifteen miles she had estimated. We reached the oil-top eventually, however, and turned off. We could see in the distance the house where we had found the dead calves. To our relief, there were no dead cows visible near the road, which made us think that our services had come in time for most of the herd.

The Londowns' house was nearer the road, readily visible, and its column of smoke rose plumb-straight into the cold, still air. I wished them luck, as we passed, feeling that such determined people were quite capable of looking after themselves. The next turnoff was Nellie's. The house was hidden behind thick privet hedges, but we could see the top of its chimney over the bushes. I watched the dash, now, and when we neared a mile, I began to look for the big hickory that marked the Fanchers' turnoff. It was impossible to miss. The thing must have been eight feet through at the base.

We bumped gently down the cross-laid-pole drive. Obviously, nobody had driven out of it in a vehicle in weeks. Through a belt of young pines, down a slope, around an arm of the wood that thrust itself into the cleared ground, we followed the drive.

Then we saw the fence, and we stopped and honked twice. We waited for a minute, then we got out of the Plymouth and walked toward the gate, very slowly.

I could feel eyes on me. Nobody was in sight, but there was the feel of vigilance all around us, and we stopped at the gate and waited. In a bit, there was a stir of motion in the garden beyond the fence. A dark face peered from behind a row of plum trees, then a tall black man stepped forward and spoke.

"Where're the Sweetbriers?" he asked in a slow, still voice. "That's their car, where are they?"

Zack moved very cautiously "Nellie is at our house," he said. "Jess is—dead. Are you Bill?"

"Dead? Really dead?" The man's eyes widened, and his

color was suddenly grayish. "How?"

"The Ungers;" Zack answered simply. "They all but killed Nellie, too. If we hadn't come down the river looking for neighbors, she'd have died that night, I think, from the cold and loss of blood."

"Come in the house," Fancher whispered, opening the gate. "We thought they were just after us because we're black. You mean they killed Jess Sweetbrier, a sweet old man like him?"

"Beat him to death," I said, as I entered the kitchen of the big gray house. I found myself facing a tall young woman who held a shotgun pointed at my midriff.

"They're all right, Annie," her husband called from behind us. She slowly lowered the gun barrel, but her expression was watchful. I could see no trace of the many children that Nellie had mentioned, but I felt that the older of them were probably in strategic locations, most likely with weapons. These people had learned caution in a tough school.

It took a while to fill them in on the state of things along the river. They had their few head of cattle penned between their barn and the road, fearing panthers more than any unlikely wanderer, so they had no need to go down to the water except in summer. No well-worn trail marked a way up to their house from the wild woods along the Oheinich. So it was that the Ungers had come at them along the road, to which they had likely made their way from the Sweetbriers'. It had never occurred to the Fanchers that the river was the direction from which they made their destructive way.

That made us uneasy. If the road had led them to the Fanchers, it would lead them to the Jessups, possibly the Greens, and inevitably to Sim Jackman. Though the Fanchers had been armed and on guard, it was unlikely that the others might be.

"I'm goin' with you," Bill told us, when we rose to pursue our investigations. "These folks along here have been right with us. They stood by us when we talked to the Law about Claude Barron's threats and stunts. They came by now and again to see how we were. We're not real close, 'cause say what you will, we're black and they're white, but we've been good neighbors, just the same. If they're in trouble, I'm goin' to be there to help 'em out."

Annie nodded, her smoky eyes still and reserved. "We're okay, the kids and I. We all know what we're doing. You just be careful, Old Son." The note in her voice said many things that her closed face hid.

As we made our way from the garden, Bill raised his hand. A thin boy appeared from behind a shed, leaned his shotgun against the building, and approached us.

"Tony, you take care of your mom and the young ones, you hear?" his father told him. The boy, not more than eleven, if that, was serious but not at all nervous. He nodded quietly, then gave me a shy grin as he turned to resume whatever chore his father had interrupted.

The mile to the Jessups' cattle guard went quickly, for along this stretch the road lay between cleared fields, and no timber was down. The chinquapin trees curved gracefully over the drive, backed by thickets of huckleberry and haw, and we went down the road looking at every turn to see the house appear, but it was a good quarter of a mile before that happened.

It was a sprawling structure of fieldstone that rose from its ridge with the authority of something that belonged just there and no place else. I knew without asking that the Jessups had built it themselves...probably grubbing the stone out of their own high-ground fields. There was smoke rising from the chimney.

The last part of the drive lay over an embankment. It was obvious that the wet fall had put the river up well into the low ground that it spanned, for there were wet patches still shining with water, and swirled debris patterned the slope of the ridge.

As we came into the open, we honked the horn, feeling that in this new world it was the fair—and safe—thing to do. Warning strangers of your approach was getting to be an ingrained habit. It was just as well that we did. A shot was fired across our bows as we crawled up the slope onto the embankment.

We stopped promptly and opened the doors. Zack and Bill got out, and I scooted across and stood beside them. We held our hands away from our sides, so they could see that we weren't holding weapons.

"Is that Bill Fancher?" came a booming voice from the shelter of a hedge.

"Sure is, Mr. Jessup," Bill answered. "These here is the Hardemans from upriver. They've come all the way round by the road to see if the folks along here are all right. The Ungers got Jess Sweetbrier a couple of days ago. If the Hardemans hadn't come down the river checking on livestock, Nellie'd have died, too."

There was a short silence. I had the feeling that a conference was going on, and evidently I was correct, for a woman's voice called, "Come on over—on foot. We don't want to seem inhospitable, but you know we've got to be careful."

"No problem," Bill called, and we went, single file, across the driveway and up the rise to the house.

Carrie Jessup was sixtyish, small and strong-looking, with wrinkles at the corners of her eyes that would have been deep with laughter in normal circumstances. Her husband, Horace, was tall and slender, with the innocently wondering eyes of a professor of philosophy or medieval literature. His hand, when I shook it, was another matter. Calloused to the point of horniness, it could have crushed my bones without effort.

Before we could speak, he said, in that incongruously booming voice, now damped to a rumble, "It's good of you to trouble yourselves about us. We've had problems, I'll admit.

"And poor Sim Jackman from down the road—he's all but dead. Crawled up here through the woods and fields, after those devil women got through with him...and his winter's cache of liquor. If he lives, it's not impossible that he'll be a teetotaler."

As he spoke, I turned my eyes to Mrs. Jessup, and I saw a slow tear creep from behind her glasses. She said nothing, but she turned away as if to look back the way we had come.

"Is that all the trouble you've had?" I asked him.

"No," he said, and his head tilted forward as if the weight of the words to come were too much for his thin neck. "No. They came at us...when was it, Mama? Three or four nights ago. They shot Grace..." His voice wavered away into a basso groan.

"Our oldest girl. She got here just after the blowup. Was on her way the night before it happened and was well away from Houston. She'd flunked out of school. Thank God. Laura was already here for the same reason. Thank the Lord we raised dumb kids. Our boy—we don't know. Anyway, the Ungers sent a little girl up the trail from the river. She was crying and taking on, all ragged and scratched and thin as a starved cat. There's no way we could have kept that child locked out. No way."

She fell silent, and Horace took up the tale. "We got her inside and gave her some warm milk, washed her up some, and were trying to find out who she was and what had happened to her when she pulled a big old hogleg pistol out of the little bundle she had with her—not more than nine!—and told me to open the door. I started for her. No infant is going to give me orders, gun or no. She'd have killed me, but Grace tackled her from the side and got hit instead. She's in the house, now, unconscious. We don't know..."

"Where's the child?" I asked, a chill crawling through my insides.

"In the house," he answered. "Laura grabbed that pistol as if she had done it every day of her life. She knocked the little wildcat out with the barrel of it. I think she'd have killed her, if we hadn't been there. Now we've got her tied up in the spare bedroom."

"But didn't they try to get in the house, after they heard the shot?" Zack asked.

"Huh!" grunted Horace. "They tried to break in the door, But they're a stupid bunch. Didn't even think to cover the front door, just the one on the river side. I eased out and around the corner and scattered them with bird-shot. They hightailed it out of sight, screaming and cussing and raising enough sand to raise the devil. Didn't seem to give another thought to the young'un we had inside."

"Sounds typical," I said, as we entered the arched doorway, into which a heavy and evidently handcrafted oak panel had been swung.

The house was as warm, down-to-earth, and pleasant on

the inside as it had seemed from a distance. Hooked rugs made puddles of color here and there on the hardwood floor that ran in a long expanse from front to back, encompassing the long living-work-dining room and the kitchen, brick-floored and wide-hearthed.

On a couch that had been pulled up beside the living-room fireplace lay a young woman who looked about fifteen, but, being Grace, must have been nearer to twenty. She was terribly pale, and the skin about her temples was bluish, as were the shadows under her cheekbones. I bent over her as we entered and laid my hand to her forehead. It was clammy.

"We have had her covered, warm bricks to her feet, the fire going full tilt," her mother said, "but she still seems to be in shock. The wound is clean—went right through the muscle of her right arm, near the shoulder."

Bill looked down at the unconscious girl. "Have you got any salt water down her?" he asked.

"Salt...water?" Carrie said doubtfully. "No. Does that help in a case of shock?"

"Can't hurt," he answered, going to the kitchen and peering into a bucket that evidently contained clean water. "This all right to drink?"

"It's out of the deep well," Horace said. "Here, let me get you the salt. And the water in the kettle is warm." He drew an old-fashioned camp kettle from the edge of the coals in the hearth.

When we had finagled several small draughts of the mixture down Grace's throat, we left her mother to continue the process and went to check on Sim Jackman. He was the most terrible sight I saw during all the time of transition. Bruised purple-to-black over every visible inch of skin, he also sported lumps and welts that testified to the merciless use of a stick. Just as had poor Jess. It was evident that he must simply either heal or die.

As I bent over him, his eyes opened. Surrounded by discolored flesh as they were, their color was hard to determine, but they were bright and alert, for all of that. He was unable to move even his head, so swollen was he, but his lips moved, and I bent near to hear.

"Who ye be?" he whispered, and I answered him, pulling Zack forward so that he could see him, too. He tried to nod, and a spasm of pain washed across his face.

To save him effort, I told him of our enclave upriver, our expedition to free the cattle, of Jess and the Fanchers. When I was done, he waggled an eyebrow to bring me closer.

"I git well," he breathed, "'m goin' to flush out them Ungers. Not fit t' live, none of' 'em. Went down there m'self, young fool, years ago. Bad then. Worse now. Dangerous. Take keer." He stopped, drained by the effort.

I stood and looked down at him. He was the thin, wiry, tough sort that you find in the back country. With his kind, size was irrelevant. They made up in grit and vinegar what they lacked in inches. I had no doubt that he would live and give the Ungers the hell they deserved.

If, that is, we were not forced to clean out that devils' den before he could.

CHAPTER EIGHT

All in all, the Jessups were fairly well set up to ride out the winter. Though they had depended on grocery-store goods for most of their necessities for years, both had been reared on farms. They had been used to storing up food against a time of need, and their years of following the oil-fields hadn't affected their know-how. In addition to what they had put up for their own use, they had already scrounged what could be had from the Greens' adjacent estate. They had been left keys by the erstwhile owners, so that they might check on dampness in the house and such matters. As the Greens were either dead or permanently stranded in Europe, Horace and Carrie had had no qualms about the thing.

But I told them to go up the river, anyway. "There is a place there, past the Londowns', with a big bunch of cattle running free. We loosed them when we came downriver yesterday, and the house was empty. Had been since the blowup, it looked like. We saw some nice young stuff—springing heifers. That should help out."

Horace nodded. "We hadn't thought of going that far. Since Bill and the Sweetbriers had stayed put, we just assumed that everyone else had, too. We quit going out when we cleaned out the hardware store in Phelan" (this being the town nearest for those on this end of the river).

Zack and I, in that intuitive way you develop after you've been married for years, were pretty well satisfied with the Jessups' status. They were the tough older stock that had seen hardships and rough times. Laura, however, was something else. I could tell that her parents were concerned, too.

She was a pretty girl, not much past eighteen. Fair, blue-eyed. You've seen her exact duplicates on every high school campus you've ever driven by. She should have been giggling her time away with pimply boys or struggling over half-comprehended textbooks. The shock of her world's ending had frozen her...almost literally.

Her expression was almost frightening, and I could imagine the cold ferocity it must have held when she tackled the Unger child. In her present state, she was more of a liability than an asset, and I knew that her people knew that. We said nothing, nor did they, but I caught every one of us watching her covertly as we talked.

The Unger child was something else entirely. When Carrie led me into the back bedroom in which she was confined, we found her gnawing like a terrier at the ropes that held her hands secured to the bedpost. Our entry brought her head up, eyes wild as those of a trapped weasel. She smelled us. I swear it. Her nostrils widened, she gave a slight nod, and I felt a cold certainty that she would be able to identify me unerringly, even in the dark, by my personal odor. She was, literally, a wild animal.

"She's our problem. Long as she's here, they're liable to come after her. We can't seem to get through to her, and I'm scared, Laura..." Her voice trailed off, but I followed her meaning.

"We've got four children at the house," I said. "Our two are older. And there are two young ones. Might be, if we took her, it would get her folks off your necks. The other kids just might be able to communicate with her, too. You can't nurse two invalids and take care of her, too."

Carrie nodded. "It would be a big help," she said. "I've a feeling they are keeping watch on us, since we've had her. They'll see you go with her in the car, and there's no way they can know where you're going. I hope."

"They're not all that bright," I reassured her.

The child was watching with bright, uncomprehending eyes, and I felt that words, other than the most basic and functional, were foreign to her. Carefully, slowly, I moved toward her, smiling as best I could. She flinched backward to the extent of her bound arms, and I could see the flesh whiten where the ropes cut off circulation. I reached as though to touch her, but a flash of small teeth warned me, and I snatched my hand away just in time. With a movement quick as a cat, she snapped at me, her teeth clicking together with the force of her intended bite.

We backed away cautiously, as if she could have sprung free and attacked us from the rear, had we turned our backs. As the door closed, Carrie looked up at me and said, "You're sure you want to tackle...that?"

"I don't want to, that's for sure, but I can't for the life of me see using any of the alternatives. She's human. She seems to be healthy...even bright, if you take her lack of teaching into account. We don't know anything at all about the rest of the country...how many are alive or what condition they're in. She's part of the future of the race, if we can tame her."

"My word," Carrie breathed. "You have thought it out the long way, haven't you? We've just been trying to see our way through this winter. The future has had to take care of itself."

"I have a son," I said, simply.

She laughed loud and long, as we went into the kitchen. Zack, though he looked at me warily, agreed to try taming the little Unger. "We don't have enough to do." He grinned. "We need a juvenile delinquent to liven things up around the place."

Then he turned to the Jessups, saying, "Can you manage two invalids? We could take Sim with us, if you want."

"I think it'd be too painful," Horace boomed. "He can hardly bear to be touched or to move at all. Jouncing that far in a car would be more than he could take. No, we'll manage. He's not a bit of trouble, really. If we can only get Grace to come around."

Bill broke in with, "I don't think it's shock. Not after all this time. She lost some blood, but not that much, and as far as I can tell the wound is fine. I've been counting it up, and it's just been too long for shock to last. I think she's withdrawn from the whole situation. Getting shot gave her the chance she needed. I've seen the same thing happen, when I was in 'Nam. Keep her warm, feed her when you can get her to eat, and when her mind figures it can cope again, she'll wake up."

Zack looked at Bill with new respect. "No wonder you're so good at setting up an armed camp. I learned things over there that I hope I'll never have to use."

"We all did," Fancher grunted, "So I guess, when you come down to the last line, it had some use, after all. It's kept the Ungers from doing more than annoy us."

It was now past noon, as I could see from the wide window that faced west toward the driveway. Though we knew that we need go no farther down the road, I had a hankering to go to its end and to see the remains of Sim Jackman's lair. I had a hunch that he had squirreled away a lot of things that the Ungers wouldn't recognize as valuable, and I wanted to check it out. Zack agreed, for the Jessups said it was only about another three miles.

"We'll stop by for a minute on our way back," he told Carrie as we left. Bill decided to wait there, helping Horace with splitting some heavy backlogs while we were gone, so Zack and I got into the stout old Plymouth and took off down toward the road's end.

When we came to the Greens' ornate gateway, we could see past it to the end of the oil-top surfacing ahead. The recent rains had softened the mud road beyond it, but no traffic had churned it up, so we put the car in low and crawled forward with caution. Aside from sliding majestically halfway round, now and again, we had no trouble. We were both born and brought up on clay-mud roads, learned to drive on them, and had never found anything we couldn't drive through since.

The woods had been cut over many times. Straggly pin oak and sweetgum stood up through the careless mess that loggers usually leave behind. Still, as we crept farther, we could see big woods ahead. We found the reason when we came to a sign that said, "Jackman's Place. Loggers will be shot." And somewhere the old devil had found a skull (it looked real) and fastened it against the big white oak that loomed over the sign.

The track that the road had degenerated into curled

through these woods lovingly, avoiding big trees that must have been young when the Indians roamed the Oheinich. Twilight lived here, even though most of the afternoon was still before us. The way ended on a knoll crowned with the biggest native magnolia I've ever seen. Seventy feet tall, if it was an inch, it spread its stiff, green-lacquered leaves above a hut that looked as if it might have grown where it stood, like a toadstool.

The door was completely off its hinges. The front wall was stove in, showing raw splinters where the wood had shattered. Tin cans and rags and nameless debris were scattered all over the little clearing, together with bits of old furniture. Nothing that would break was in one piece, and nothing that would tear was whole. Still, I entered the place hopefully. I couldn't see those lazy bitches going to extra effort with really tough things.

I was right. The iron cook-stove stood against the wall, unhurt in the catastrophe. A Dutch oven leaned crazily against the wall, its lid lying under a dent that would just have fitted the knob handle on its top. I started, then and there, to make a pile of things to take back to Carrie, who was making do with her cookery over the open fireplace with only light camp stuff to use.

The contents of the hut looked as if they'd been stirred with a spoon. With all the debris outside, I had thought to find it all but empty, but Sim must have accumulated "things" all his life. Under a bunch of stove-in baskets I found a real cast-iron popover pan. Before the blowup, it would have been worth a bunch to antique collectors. Now it was worth more to us.

There was a cobbler's last, with the funny-shaped hammer. These had been flung into the fireplace. All in all, Sim had a treasure trove, and I had a Plymouth-load almost before Zack had finished taking down the stovepipe and getting the cook-stove ready so that the Jessups could move it right out.

When we got back to the stone house, it was getting late. We hurriedly unloaded a pile of iron utensils, which Carrie received with groans of pleasure. When we added the news of the cook-stove, she turned to Horace.

"The old pickup—it'll still run, if we use the battery off the Ford. Tomorrow we've got to go down and get that thing, if we break both our backs. I've had a blistered face for almost two months now, and I'm ready for a change."

Bill Fancher grinned. "Long about eight o'clock, I'll come over and go with you to help you load and unload. We've got plenty of cooking stuff, but there's likely some old axe heads and such that I could fix up to use. I'd like to take a look around there, myself."

So it was arranged, and we dropped Bill off at his house just as the sun began to sink behind the trees. It was strange, driving home along empty roads, with never a light along the way to mark someone's home. Only once, as we came over the last hill that gave an overview of the whole valley of the Oheinich, did we see, far away to our right, a tiny point of reddish light.

Our passenger rode in dead silence. She had entered the car with terror, her eyes rolled back like those of a spooked horse, and once we had her secured to the seat, she had sat, tense and wary, making no sound. I turned, now and again, to speak to her, but she seemed not to be used to having words addressed to her. I had a sneaky idea that what instruction she had had taken the form of slaps and harder blows.

When we turned into the yard of home, I looked back and said, "This will be your home, now. There are other children here. Nobody is going to hurt you if you behave yourself. Don't bite. Don't try to kill anybody. If you do, we'll have to keep you tied up."

Uncomprehending silence answered me.

The Savonius, with its banks of batteries salvaged from the phone-company warehouse, had become so familiar to us that we never thought of the effect of electric lights on a child who had probably never seen them, even before the blowup. The brightly lighted kitchen window drew her gaze, and she stared with hypnotic intensity while we bundled out the wares that I had kept from Sim's store. When she realized that we were going to take her into the house that was lighted with that eerie illumination, she shrieked like a calliope.

That brought out the troops, sure enough. Jim, peering into the back seat of the car, where his father and I were struggling with the wild young creature, touched me on the shoulder. "Mom," he whispered, "why don't you try letting Sukie do it?"

Zack and I looked at one another in the dim light, then we nodded. Sukie crawled into the other side as we wriggled out on the driver's. She sat there for a short time, simply looking at the other child. For the first time, I realized that the past weeks had matured my children incredibly. Sukie was sizing up the situation, gauging the exact depth of the little Unger's terror and rage, and deciding her own strategy in dealing with it. Though she was more than a year younger than the other, she seemed almost adult by comparison.

Then she reached over and loosed the knots that we had tied, out of our captive's reach, in order to hold her in her seat. When the ropes were off, Sukie took the grubby hand she had freed and helped the child from the car, never saying a word. Something that she was projecting toward the wild little creature was calming her.

Though her eyes were still glazed with fear, the girl came into the brightly lighted kitchen compelled only by the touch of Sukie's fingers on her arm. The smell of roasting meat and baking cornbread brought her to full awareness. Then it was only a matter of feeding her until she could hold no more, wiping the tears and food stains from her face and hands, and putting her to bed. She was so soundly asleep by that time that she had no idea of what was happening. We put her on a cot in the pantry, securing the door from outside as a precaution. Food and rest might well send her into new efforts at murder and sudden death.

Sukie sat at the supper fable, wordless and thoughtful. I leaned over the table and patted her shoulder.

"I'm proud of you," I said. "But what did you do? And how did you make her understand, without talking to her?"

Sukie looked at me patiently. "She's just like the young coon we caught. Don't you remember? Its eyes looked just the same. It didn't know anything about words, either. I got it to stop trying to throw itself through the walls of the pen, and I did it just the same way. I...felt at it. All sort of sleepy and soft and relaxed. It worked."

Behind me, Zack sighed. Then he sat down, his cup of comfrey tea steaming, and cut a hot wedge of cornbread. "Makes me feel old," he said to us all, stirring honey into his cup. "When my own baby has more gumption than I do, it just purely makes me feel old...but good." He took a scalding sip and grinned at Sukie, and she grinned back at him.

Mom Allie chuckled. "Now you're beginning to understand how I feel," she said wryly. "But it's going to take more than feeling at that young'un to civilize her. Don't anybody have any ideas about that?"

We all sat and pondered. Then Jim's eyes lit up like Christmas trees. Exactly like Christmas trees.

"It's not long until Christmas," he said, "Maybe if we...one last time...put lights on the tree and all our old pretty things...I'll bet she's never seen anything pretty, let alone gorgeous like Mom can make a tree look. This last time that there'll be enough bulbs to light it up right, let's do it up right. We've got the tree cut already...it's soaking out by the porch right now...let's see if it won't...do something..."

Though he was only marginally coherent, we all saw the possibilities at once. Christmas was a time for miracles, anyway. Perhaps we might wring one last miracle from it, with the aid of our scrounged-up power system.

For a little while each night, we decided, a wisp of the old, lost world would intrude into this harsh new existence.

CHAPTER NINE

We had moved in such a fury of concentrated effort in the time since early November that we had taken little thought of the approaching season. Mom Allie had knitted new mittens for the children—all four of them. Zack had whittled some knickknacks from seasoned hickory. We had spent most of our time thinking of surviving, however, and the Christmas magic hadn't really percolated through us with all its old fervor. Even when the children had brought in a stout little pine tree and set it to soak in a tub, we had noticed with only part of our minds.

Now the season took on an extra dimension. In addition to its closeness of feeling, we hoped from it something very strange. For, in truth, if this didn't wedge open a chink in the heart of the child we had fallen heir to, we had no idea what, if anything, ever could.

Not that we had time or inclination to give our all to the celebration. A spell of good weather sent us into the fields, breaking the stubble of last year into the soil and turning it to catch the winter rains. The horses were used for plowing, along with Maud (to all their intense disgusts), for we had scrounged enough plow tools to keep three teams busy. Jim was tall enough to do his first plowing, under the tutelage of Maud; Sukie, measuring herself against the plow handles, swore that by next fall she'd be tall enough to do it too.

The child was a problem. We named her Lisa for no good reason other than the fact that we had to call her something. She was quiet as death, most of the time. It's true that she began to realize that "Lisa" was directed only toward her, and she would duck her head when she heard the name.

But she still flinched when anything at all came at her fast, particularly at head height. She seemed puzzled that we didn't beat her, too, though we watched her too closely to let her get into mischief.

Still, we couldn't really trust her to stay in the house alone, even though she had shown no inclination toward running back to her erstwhile "family." Then Sukie solved the problem of what to do with Lisa while we were in the fields. We put her on the back of one of the horses. Her weight was negligible, she was delighted—as far as we could tell from her enigmatic face—and we could keep an eye on her without looking away from our work.

For three days we worked to get some of the fields in order. Then, four days before Christmas, a howling norther blew in, bringing freezing rain, sleet, hail, volleys of snow, and an end to outside work for a time. The children took their well-soaked tree from its tub, set it in our old tree stand, and bore it into the front room.

Lisa watched uncomprehendingly as they decided just where to put it, arranged it to their exact specifications, then bustled the Christmas boxes down from the closet in the loft. She edged nearer as they opened the boxes (themselves antiques, some of them) and began taking out the hanks of tinsel, the fragile glass balls, the handmade "cookie" ornaments.

Zack strung the lights out (his inevitable method) and began putting bulbs in the sockets, noting sadly that we had very few extras. As the first light winked green, then one flashed red, one blue, the child's eyes grew wide with astonishment. She inched forward until she almost touched the string, watching each new bulb inserted with rapt attention. Zack casually handed her a red one. She looked at it, watched as he put one more in its socket, then set the bulb in its place and began screwing it carefully.

Her concentration was such that she didn't notice when the lot of us stopped work to observe the operation. When the red light leaped into being, she sat back, the veneer of her face cracked wide open and pure joy beaming forth. "Ooohh!" she crowed, and it was the first sound other than a scream or a growl that I had ever heard her make.

She looked around at all of us. Nine smiles as large as her own met her gaze (Miss Vera was visiting for the occasion). She blushed almost as red as her light and scuttled back into her corner, where I had put two fat cushions for her exclusive use. There she stayed, as the other four children decorated the tree, to constant advice from the adults on the sidelines.

Zack disconnected the lights while they put them on the tree. Then we waited while the glittering ornaments were attached (with much disagreement as to whether they were properly balanced). When the last plastic icicle (they glowed in thc dark) was hung, the star firmly affixed to the top, Zack plugged in the lights.

I didn't watch the tree. I kept my eyes on Lisa. And I wasn't disappointed. The tree didn't light up one bit more than she did.

We moved about it, exclaiming that it was, in purest truth, the prettiest ever. That it was probably the last of its exact kind was a thought that nobody uttered. Future trees might have lights, but they would grow fewer and fewer until all the bulbs were burned out.

When we had agreed that nothing at all needed changing, we unplugged it. There was a wail from Lisa's corner.

Zack bent over her. "Tonight, for thirty minutes, we'll turn it back on. We'll put all the other lights out and just sit and enjoy the tree. Okay?"

She looked up at him. "Okay," she whispered.

A moment of silence followed. It was, I guessed, the first time in her short life that she had verbally answered a question. It could have been the first time that her mind was not too blocked with terror to comprehend the question that was asked. It was, without doubt, a milepost in our relationship with her.

Then we came to ourselves, subdued our smiles to a decent level, and went about cleaning up the mess we had made. Lisa sat on one of her cushions, her eyes alert and a strange expression about her mouth. In anyone else, it would have been the beginning of a smile, but Lisa was not used to such facial gymnastics. The wide grin that had come with her red light was the first true expression that we had ever caught on her face.

It seemed a long time before darkness fell, even though the gray day should have cut the daylight short. We puttered with small chores, engaged in teasing and tale-telling, wandered into and out of the room where the tree stood. Supper was early, just to help kill time. But at last the windows made glossy mirrors against the blackness outside, and the time had come to light the tree again.

Lisa had eaten absently. Her face was closed again, her eyes veiled. When we had cleared away the food and cleaned the dishes, we called the children to come into the living room to help light the tree. She came almost reluctantly. The glow of the lights filled the room with magic, as it always had. I stood with one arm around Zack, the other around Mom Allie, and I stole a peep to catch the miniature tree sparkling in her glasses, twinned, as I used to do with my own parents. The moment took me back into the deeps of childhood, for an instant, and I shivered with the nameless anticipation that the season had always brought to me.

The children were sitting on the rug in an arc before the tree. Sam was sitting, solid and square, between Jim, whose thin figure tingled with excitement, and Sukie, who glowed between him and Candy. Lisa had returned to her cushions and was beyond the range of my vision. We didn't talk, we only sat and looked (or stood and looked) and enjoyed.

A strangled sob interrupted us. From Lisa's corner the gulping cry brought us all about. She was bent over, the pillow in her arms, her face buried in its embroidered bosom. Her shoulders heaved with the force of her crying. I was there almost before I knew that I had moved.

I touched her shoulder hesitantly, but there was no sign of the instant pulling-away she had always showed. I picked her up, cushion and all, and carried her to my rocking chair, where I sat with her in my lap. She wept like a man, deep, racking convulsions. Not the easy tears of a child or a woman. Her thin body shook in my arms until Zack came and knelt beside the rocker, putting his arms around both of us. Encircled so, Lisa's shaking eased, and the tears flowed more naturally.

I took the cushion from her arms, very gently, and held

her head against my shoulder. Her arms crept about my neck, quite timidly, and she tucked her wet cheek against my throat. Her other hand grasped Zack's arm.

There in the dim and magical light of the Christmas tree, I smiled at my husband. He smiled back. Outside our small world, the greater world might lie in chaos. Mankind might be cast far back along the road we had so painfully traveled. Here there was life, there was love. Here, for a time at least, some of the values that had been the crown of our age were still alive and working.

Early though it was, I washed Lisa's tear-stained face and put on her flannel nightgown. Then I took her into her cubbyhole and laid her in her cot. I sat beside her until she hiccupped herself to sleep. Then I tiptoed out, my own eyes dampish. For the first time, I didn't latch the pantry door.

We sat, that evening, in the dim, warm light of the tree. Not one of us felt the need to read or to sew, to play a game or to do anything that required bright light. It was as if the wonderful thing that had happened in our midst had us caught still in its spell, and we feared that we might rupture that brightness if we unplugged the tree and turned on the reading lamps.

We talked quietly, letting the warmth flow through us, letting our spirits grow calm and still. When bedtime came, we took turns for warm baths, and, of course, I waited until last of all.

Soaking in the tub, I thanked God that we had provided so well for all our needs. The abandoned refrigerator, coupled with a burned-out water-heater core, augmented the warmed water that flowed about the firebox of our cookstove and on into the pipes, giving us an ample supply. We didn't have tubsful to soak in, but five gallons of really hot water can provide a bath fit for a king. The sun and the plentiful wood supply did the work that so many had worried about for so long in our recurring "energy crises."

The bad weather continued for three days, and Christmas Eve found us better prepared for the event than we had thought possible. Though the older children, even Sam, had settled the Santa Claus issue, baby Candy was agog. The others, with the grave courtesy that well-reared children can show, hung their stockings beside hers and talked excitedly about what they might expect to get in them.

When the loft was full of children who if not asleep were at least in bed, Lucas and Skinny, Josh and Elmond, Lantana and Miss Vera came through the moonlit frost of the night, their arms burdened with large parcels. Rag dolls emerged from the bundles. Wooden soldiers with jointed arms and legs that held them upright on flat black-paint boots. Scarves and caps knitted from the wools that we had garnered in town. Acorn and hickory-nut-hull dishes and manikins. The old people had used the bad weather well, and there was enough for more than five children.

Lisa had hung her long sock beside the others, saying nothing but puzzled past words. Her speech was coming, now, with fair regularity, but the questions in her face were too big for her short supply of language. I took special joy in stuffing her sock full of small, bright things. I topped it with a joyous homemade Raggedy Ann.

We woke to a glorious morning. The sun was just illuminating the frost-filigreed weeds and branches and pine needles outside the windows, whose shutters we had opened, when Candy came down the chilly steps from the loft. She was barefoot, and she was demanding loudly to see her "'tockin'."

The others were just behind her, their blasé attitudes wiped out entirely by the reality of Christmas morning. They waited impatiently while we shod Candy, then all five (Lisa having emerged from her cubby) went into the living room in a bunch. Zack had gone before and plugged in the tree. The fire was crackling in the heater. The stockings were ranged along the back of the couch, where they had been pinned the night before. Now they stood stiff as Guardsmen, against the cushions.

There was a concerted "Ooooh!"

Jim and Sukie, Sam and Candy fell upon their treasures and began digging into them. Lisa stood before hers in utter surprise. Raggedy Ann grinned at her, her black button eyes sprinkled with colored reflections. Timidly, the child grinned back.

"Take her out, honey," Zack whispered. "She's yours.

All yours."

With terrible slowness, Lisa drew the doll from the tight-fitting stocking, held her up, turned her about to admire the bow that tied her apron. She suddenly hugged her close to her thin chest. With much care, she tucked the bright yarn head against her in what I realized suddenly was exactly the way I had held her the night before. My eyes misted, and I turned them to the antics of the other children.

Each of them, from Candy to Jim, sat in a circle of items of varying degrees of brightness, usefulness, or simple interest. Their faces were...surprised.

Zack took my hand. "If I'd thought about it, I would have said that we'd have no time nor energy for any Christmas doings, now that we're strictly on our own. But it's not true. I remember, now, that my granddad used to tell me about the fine Christmases they had when he was little. A few handmade toys, clothes that his mother had made from the basic cotton and wool to the finished things. A lot of love and ingenuity and make-do. He remembered it all his life, the magic his parents used to make, likely taking all year's odd moments to do it. This may be the last tree with colored lights, Luce, but we'll have a tree as long as we're able to go out and cut one."

"And we'll make Christmas for the children, and they'll do it for theirs...if we survive," I added.

Then our other household descended on us, anxious to learn the effect of their long hours of work. None were disappointed. The small things we adults had made for one another were opened and admired, but Christmas, we learned again, is seen through the eyes of children.

And Lisa, her doll tight against her shoulder, her pockets stuffed with strung-acorn dolls and teacups made of hickory-nut hulls, opened like a flower, her thin body seeming almost to grow rounder with the fullness of her happiness. She spoke, now and again, breathless monosyllables that we took turns in answering, whether they made sense or not.

Our Christmas feast was a bit odd. Baked hen and cornbread dressing, with every sort of vegetable, centered the table, of course. But the bright cranberries, the exotic olives that had always been a part of it, were as inaccessible as if they had existed on another planet. Nuts and stewed dried fruit filled in nicely, but I felt an uncontrollable twinge as I thought of the things that I had known as part of my life that our descendants would never know, save as tales out of our youth.

Then I thought of the things that had been twisted and warped, the things that we had fled from when we left Houston. Those, too, were gone, just as irrevocably. I smiled about the table. My husband, my children, my mother-in-law, and my friends who were fast becoming family smiled back, and I wouldn't have changed a thing that had happened in the past weeks, even if I could have.

CHAPTER TEN

With the turning of the year, new vigor seemed to surge in all of us, as well as in the soil underfoot. Even Nellie Sweetbrier mended quickly and was able to wander about the nearer wood and the gardens, looking for wild edibles to transplant, planning rows of vegetables to come. And, in truth, we all felt the sap beginning to flow again.

Those in the unfortunate North must wait until spring to begin their farming, but here we break garden ground in January, the weather permitting, and plant greens and radishes and lettuce and many things that germinate in cool ground. And we were fortunate in the new year. The bitter weather that had raked November and part of December gave way to warm days and nights just chilly enough to be brisk.

While Lantana, Mom Allie, Miss Vera, Suzi, Nellie, and I took turns turning the gardens behind the fat pony, the men were breaking ground for corn. The breeze came from the south, balmy in midday, and the soil crumbled richly to the plows. Now we knew that we must scrounge in earnest. We had saved seed corn, the old-fashioned flint variety that bred true.

But we had had no way to know that it must serve so many, or that there would be no way to buy any more. Lucas and Skinny put their heads together and came up with four names. "Arthur Simkins, Lanny Bushing, Teddy Bolt, and Lemuel Satterwhite raise lots of popcorn and Indian corn," Lucas said.

"They've always held a lot for seed. If they're there, we can trade honey or alcohol or canned stuff for it. If they're not...well, it's not the same world that it was."

So Miss Vera and I went scrounging for seed-corn, taking the pickup, which we had finally adapted to burn alcohol. That being in good supply, because of the ample supply of acorns, hickory nuts, spoiled corn, and such that we continually fed into the fermenting buckets, we carried extra in five-gallon milk cans that we had salvaged from one of the abandoned dairies up the road. Whether we might need it for trading or for refueling we didn't know, but it felt good to have it along.

The roads had gone wild in those few weeks. In places, so much debris had blown onto the asphalt that it was invisible for as much as forty feet. Branches, loose grass, and dirt that had washed about in the flooding we had experienced, even trees, made a weird tangle of the road that had, two months before, been exceptionally smooth and well cared for. We used the chain saw several times in order to go through.

The Bolt farm was south of us, Miss Vera said. As she knew every man, child, and dog that lived anywhere in the county or ever had, I followed her directions, and we arrived safely at a mailbox that was labeled rather fancifully with a large bolt run through a flange welded to its top. Smoke was coming from the chimney of the house, and we smiled at one another as we bumped down the washed-out driveway toward the square frame house.

Before we had gone halfway, a lanky figure had started up the drive to meet us. Though there was a wide grin on his face, Bolt carried a ten-gauge shotgun in the crook of his arm. When he saw Miss Vera's round face, though, he gave a loud whoop, and a short, dumpy woman came out into the open, setting down her own shotgun to come forward and greet us as we jounced to a stop.

"Hellfire!" he yelled. "Josie, it's Vera! Thought she'd be dead an' gone, with all the rest of the folks we knew. But here she is, sound as a dollar."

"Teddy," grunted his wife, "you're a fool. The dollar doesn't even exist anymore. Sound as a dollar! Sound as a hickory nut, maybe. Not a dollar!"

So, squabbling amiably, they escorted us from the car

into their house. It was the sort of shoddily built shanty that most of the poorer people have lived in as long as I can remember. You could see out of cracks around the window frames. The door sagged so that a wedge of sky showed above one corner. The room was hot, however, from the ferocious blaze on the dinky brick hearth.

When we stated our errand, Teddy Bolt's face grew even redder than its normal turkey-gobbler hue. "Alcohol! Lord, I'd give anything I've got, 'cept Josie, for a drink of good old white lightnin'. Sure, I've got more seed-corn than I can ever plant for just the two of us. Alcohol."

"Theodore!" snapped Miss Vera, "this is fuel alcohol, not drinkin' alcohol. You drink this stuff and you'll look like your great-uncle Robert that had the jack-leg when he was young, from moonshine. If you live, that is. We make a little good stuff for medicine and such, but the stuff that comes out of the barrels would kill a goat."

His face fell, and Josie grinned unsympathetically. "Got nothin' to burn it in," she chuckled. "You have anythin' else to trade?"

"Honey and canned goods," I said.

Both their faces broke into grins. "Honey! We've intended for years to get us some bees, but never seemed to get around to it. We'll trade you corn all day and all night for a good jug of honey."

"A gallon do?" asked Miss Vera, and both nodded vigorously. So the deal was made, and we left the Bolts behind, bickering happily over who would make the biscuits to spread the honey on. I met nobody else, then or ever, who lived so nearly as they always had, without fear of the present or worry about the future. They paid us a visit, a year later, riding two spavined mules that must have taken a full week to cover the forty miles between our farms, and they were no older, no sadder, no wiser than they had been on that first visit. They were perfect examples of the best and the worst of the "po' white trash" that so many had labored for so long to bring into the mainstream of ambition, ulcers, and money. They were healthy, tough, and durable, and they'll die as they've lived, in their own way and at their own time.

Miss Vera had routed us in a large arc, so as to make all

the farms we needed to make contact with, yet avoid back-tracking. The Satterwhites were west of us, northwest of the Bolts. We rattled and rumbled over mud roads that were no better and no worse than ever, as they were always just short of impassable. We snaked back and forth, up and down hills, and when we hit Highway 69 we were less than five miles from the place we were aiming for.

There was a white gate, closed across a neatly graveled drive. In the distance we could see an immaculately white house, low and many-windowed beneath its green roof. No sign of life moved about it, no smoke curled from the stone chimney. We opened the white gate and crept down the drive cautiously, in case anyone there might be trigger-happy.

No one was. Not a living soul was on the place, though there was enough wood cut for the winter, the root cellar was full, and in the fields behind the house cattle scrounged through the winter-killed grass. The door wasn't locked, and Miss Vera, with the self-confidence of her age and class, tapped once, yoo-hooed, and walked in.

She walked back out immediately, her face white.

"Somebody's in there...dead. Mighty dead. I don't want to know. Let's go look in the crib in the barn." She turned on her heel.

The barn was tidier than my house usually stays. Everything was whitewashed that would hold still for it, all the woodwork was in good repair, and even the corncrib was clean. No cobwebs festooned the corners, no felted layers of dust lay on the piles of bags in the corners. The seed-corn was in coarse white bags, labeled clearly "field corn" and "colored Indian corn."

We took a bag of each, feeling like thieves, even though we well knew that whoever came to live here again would not be a Satterwhite and would never know or care that part of the seed-corn was gone. While I manhandled the bags to the truck, Miss Vera, in her indomitable way, poked about the barn, then went into the stables.

Once again, her curiosity got her into trouble. I heard a stifled cry and dropped the last bag into the pickup, then hot-footed it for the stable. In the gloom I could see her round figure coming toward me, and her face was, again, white.

"It's Amos. Ella must have died of something, there in the house. When she was gone, Amos came out here and..." She gestured.

In the corner a long figure swayed from a beam. As my eyes grew accustomed to the dimness, I could see that it was a man of about sixty. He had been so thin that even the bloat of death hadn't made him look much larger than he had in life. The scent of the alfalfa hay stored along the wall muted the stink until it was little noticeable—or perhaps Amos had been so emaciated that there wasn't anything left to smell.

Two months before, I would have been profoundly shaken. Now I looked at him, looked at Miss Vera, and asked, "Do you want me to bury him?"

She shook her head. "I wouldn't feel right about doing him and not doing Ella. And she...she'd be a terrible chore. As the Bible says, let the dead bury the dead. I never understood that before. Now I know."

I took her plump arm, and through it I could feel the deep quiver that shook her short frame. Putting my arm about her shoulders, I said, "Look at it this way, Miss Vera. They don't have to worry about anything. They're safe, now."

We climbed into the pickup and slammed the balky doors. Then she looked at me and a quavery smile crooked her mouth. She picked up her list of names and drew a firm line through Satterwhite. A vigorous check mark had tallied the Bolts. I hoped that we would find no more to line through before the day ended.

It was noon. Lantana had urged a lunch bag upon us, but after our last stop we found no appetite for it. That turned out to be a good thing. As we moved cautiously down the cluttered road, Vera suddenly cried, "Stop!"

Obediently, I stopped, and she motioned for me to back up. I halted again before an unpainted shack—what they used to call a shotgun house, because all the rooms were in one line, like the load of a shotgun shell. Now I could see a small face at the window, and I hurried after Miss Vera up the path worn through dead grass burrs.

When we called, there was a fumbling at the door, but whoever did it was either too young or too weak to open it. I heaved, and the flimsy thing gave way. We faced a little black girl who must have been less than five, though she was so thin it was hard to tell. On a pallet in the corner were three other children, one little more than an infant. They were alive, but only just, and one of them was breathing so raggedly through chest congestion that it sounded as though it was shaking the floor.

"Is anybody else here?" I asked the girl, and she shook her head.

"Pa, he lef' us here, say he gone for he'p. Never come back. We so hungry!"

I tore out for the truck and came back with the bag of lunch. In consideration of Miss Vera's uncomfortable dentures, Lantana had packed several biscuits that had been buttered while hot and soaked in honey. Those went into the listless mouths of the younger ones, while the girl, LaTonsha, chunked into the roast pork and cornbread that had been put in for me. The infant was a problem. Finally, I soaked one of the biscuit bits in water until it was a watery mush. Then Miss Vera spooned it into the baby while I held him.

When everything edible was gone, we cleaned them up as well as we could with rags and water, wrapped them in the pieced quilt off the bed in the second room, and packed them into the truck between us. There was no question of going on. These children must be gotten to the house as fast as possible, and I retraced our way so that we'd lose no time in cutting away more fallen trees and debris from a new set of roads.

We were home before mid-afternoon. Zack was still working in the far field with Lucas and Elmond. Only Suzi and Mom Allie were in the house, for the children had gone to scrounge the last few hickory nuts and acorns along the creek.

When we started unloading little black children, Mom Allie came bustling out of the house with Suzi just behind her. "Lord have mercy!" she whispered. "These pore little things. Look starved to death. Let's boil a chicken, Suzi. Go catch one and kill it. I'll dress it while you help Luce get all these kids settled down."

Miss Vera, for all her seeming vigor, had had a killing day. We put her to bed in Suzi's place, and we noted that she made no protest.

Then we ran the tub full of good warm water and put all four of the chilled youngsters into it. The baby we held carefully, but we let him soak until the chill left his feet and hands, and his color returned to its natural burnt-caramel color from the ash-blue that it had been. By the time we finished, the chicken was on to boil and a pot of comfrey tea was steeped.

We loaded cups of the hot beverage with honey and gave it to the now-revived older children. The baby's had a bit of milk added to it, and Mom Allie had found and boiled out the bottle we had bought for feeding an orphaned pup. That was just the ticket. The little fellow showed the first sign of real life when the nipple went between his lips, the warm brew gurgled down his throat, and his shriveled belly began to fill. We didn't let any of them have much, for they had been empty for too long. Still, you could see life pouring back into them.

As we put them to sleep on a long pallet in the loft room, we were smiling, but when we stepped back and saw the wall-to-wall sleeping place that the never-spacious loft had become, we realized that some accommodation must be made. We seemed destined to bring home waifs, and they couldn't be stood up in corners. Either we must build onto the cabin or we must provide another entire house. With the new four, there would now be eleven people crammed into our log home. As I pondered the problem, Suzi began to crack her knuckles, a sure sign that she was having ideas.

"All right, Su, what's going on in the old skull?" I asked her. "I know you're cooking up something in there."

She giggled, then said, "You know, I was thinking about how much time it would take to do any building, with time for putting in crops so very nearly"—she caught herself—"near. So why not go into one of the towns and take one or two mobile homes that are just sitting there on their wheels?"

I backed cautiously out of the narrow slot in which I stood and began retreating down the ladder. The lower I went, the better the idea looked.

When we were down in the kitchen getting supper on the table, Suzi said, “You know the steep bank to the east—the one that slants down so fast to let the roadway pass?”

I nodded.

“Why couldn’t we dig out a hole in it and push the trailer back into the bank—to keep out the cold, you know, and to keep wind from”—she thought a minute—”over-setting it?”

As that had been my only quibble with the plan, I smiled broadly. “You are hereby nominated our planner-in-chief,” I told her. “We’ll bounce it off Zack when he comes in, and Miss Vera can take it up with her household in the morning when she goes home.”

Any man who returns from a hard day’s plowing to find that his family has grown by four is in an iffy mood. We waited until he was suppered and bathed and relaxed under his reading lamp, an old issue of *Mother Earth News* on his lap. Then we proposed Suzi’s plan.

We needn’t have worried. Any plan that would have increased the floor space without taking valuable time for building would have made him happy. And in his sleep, instead of muttering “Gee!” and “Giddap!” and whacking me with his still-active elbows, he mumbled about trailers and earth-sheltered homes and sheets of vinyl to keep out the damp.

The Hardeman Home for Stranded Survivors was under way.

CHAPTER ELEVEN

Our foray into Nicholson to search out a suitable trailer was delayed for several days. Our four new members were not well, not at all. The three-year-old, Lillian, was the one with the terrible cough, and we were antsy about pneumonia. She was not only all but shaken apart by her coughing fits, but she was so frightened of being left, once again, by herself with no adult that she wasn't satisfied unless she was in somebody's lap.

La-Tonsha held her more than anyone, but the fragile five-year-old tired quickly. Lillian was almost as big as she was, and her fever made her restless. Mom Allie, Suzi, and I were called in all directions at odd moments, so that we made highly unreliable laps.

Miss Vera solved the problem when she came over to see how our charges were doing. She hadn't really recovered her vigor since our outing, and she seemed happy to sit in the old Lincoln rocker, rocking quietly and crooning old songs to the child in her high, cracked voice. There was something hypnotic in the combination. La-Tonsha and the other girl, two-year-old Jashie, would sit as near as they could get without getting pinched by the rockers...and Lisa would draw nearer and nearer until she was among the group too.

Joseph, the baby, was amazing. He was less than a year old—maybe ten or eleven months. Though he had been starved almost to the point of no return, once we had him warm and clean and eating again, he simply relaxed and took turns eating, sleeping, and trying to walk all over the house. We made playpens of turned-over chair backs. He blithely bumped them out of the way and moved on like a small bulldozer. We rigged barriers across the doors. He tugged and tugged until they gave way. He recognized nothing as impossible. As I said, an amazing child.

We kept pouring comfrey tea down the four children, with milk from Nellie Sweetbrier's goat, Tillie, who had freshened and provided us with almost two quarts of milk a day. Her twins were a couple of imps that we named Punch and Judy. Their antics, seen from the kitchen windows, were almost as good for the children as her milk was.

We began to relax when Lillian's chest stopped sounding like bagpipes. By that time, the others had recovered a bit of their spirits, and good food and plenty of cuddling when the nightmares woke them seemed to be handling things well. We arranged for Skinny Trotter and Josh Nolan, who had both been "down" with rheumatism so that they had trouble moving about, to come and stay with Nellie and the smaller child while Mom Allie, Suzi, Lantana, and I went to find supplemental housing.

Miss Vera declined to go. She had moved into our house now to be with Sam, and she sat in the rocker with one or another of the children on her lap. Even Lisa had been enticed into that plump spot, and now she took her turn, along with the small children. But Miss Vera's eyes were no longer bright and young in her wrinkled face. Now she looked farther and deeper than the surfaces she saw, and I felt a chill premonition that she would not be with us for too long now.

However, we drove off, one morning in late January, in the Plymouth, to which Zack had attached a tow bar that we had scrounged back in November. The car ran well on our home-made alcohol, and we found the roads into Nicholson to be in better shape than the lesser ones we had been traveling. To our astonishment, though, the power lines were all to pieces.

Evidently there had been windstorms during the bad weather that we hadn't realized were so strong. Or it might have been that only the constant maintenance of the T P & L crews had kept the intricate network of lines intact. However it was, the poles still stood, but the lines sagged, where they weren't all the way down.

We passed slowly through Penrose, looking in every direction for a telltale wisp of smoke, but there was nothing. All the way to Manville we wondered aloud what set of circumstances had made almost everyone leave a safe spot that was well equipped for survival to take off for parts unknown. We've never solved the riddle to our satisfaction.

Nicholson was a surprise. At the "City Limits" sign we paused to read. The "Population: 29,300" had been altered to read "950." Below that "Amos Ledbetter, Mayor" had been added in a straggly hand.

Remembering that doughty man from our first post-blowup trip to town, I entered at a very moderate rate of speed and meticulously observed every stop sign I came to. The fact that we were the only vehicle on the street would not, I felt, moderate his wrath if we didn't mind all the outdated rules that were so dear to him. It was as well I did.

We turned off the main drag to go by Mom Allie's house. There were still a few things that she wanted to pick up, and we had room in the trunk of the car. Just as I began to pick up speed again after the turn I heard the screech of a whistle blown by mighty lungs.

"Amos?" I asked Mom Allie.

"Amos," she answered, as I pulled to a halt.

"Get out of there with yo' hands up!" he shouted, as he puffed up to the car. "Damn looters 're not goin' to strip my town!"

We sat still, until Mom Allie put her window down and said sharply, "Amos, I declare, you're a worse fool every day you live. I'm goin' by my old place to get some things I left there. There aren't any looters, and if you haven't had any by now you're not goin' to. Now shut up and get on with your mayorin'."

His face fell. "Miss Alice, you really think there won't be no looters?"

"Amos," she said, less sharply, "if you got things organized here in town, all those old folks and young'uns the powers that be left to live or die in the armory out into housing, with something to eat, then you've done a pure D miracle. Don't get carried away with the idea of fightin' off gangs of bad guys; stick to the job you took on. They'll likely rename the town either Amosville or Ledbetter before you're through."

"Well," he said, his red face turning even brighter, "I have got things in better shape. I took over the Pioneer Village and put most of 'em in there and in them housekeeping apartments right next to 'em. We scrounged up enough wood cook-stoves to do us—we cook for everybody all in the same place, then take the meals to them that can't get around. The kids've jumped right in and are handy as all get-out. There's a few families that still live in their own homes, too. They had fireplaces, and we've all pitched in, them that are able, to keep firewood cut and hauled in."

"How are you fixed for fuel for the trucks?" I asked him.

"It's gettin' mighty low, he admitted. "We're goin' to have to go to haulin' stuff on our backs pretty soon."

"No way," I said, getting out of the car with Zack's brainchild in my hand. "We've rigged up stills, out our way, to use anything you can think of to ferment into alcohol. There are plans in this packet for ethanol stills, using grain and fruit and berries of all kinds, and for making methane in an airtight drum and distilling the gas into methanol. You take this and get whoever is best at tinkering. I'll bet you all are making your own fuel in less than two months. There are directions for altering carburetors to run on pure alcohol, too."

We drove off, leaving the mayor of Nicholson babbling his thanks. Mom Allie's face, however, was a study in mixed emotions.

"If I'd known what was to happen," she said, "and somebody had offered me a million to guess who it would be that would pull this town together and keep it goin', I'd never, ever, have picked Amos Ledbetter. That'll teach me to judge folks by the outside. Always been a failin' of mine. Amos Ledbetter! Well!" And she fell silent as we turned into the drive and circumnavigated the house to her rear quarters.

It took only a short time to gather up the last of her possessions. Then we headed out toward the Loop and the acres of finished mobile homes that had been parked there by the factory that adjoined the main highway into Nicholson. They sat there looking, already, a bit battered and weathered. When we looked through a few, we shook our heads. The craftsmanship was nonexistent. They were shoddy through and through.

"Let's find Amos," Mom Allie said at last. "We need a good older one that folks have lived in and kept up, but don't need anymore."

It wasn't hard to find Amos. We just went back to the spot where we had left him and leaned on the car horn. He was there in five minutes.

Once he understood what we needed (and why), he knew exactly where to go. South of town there had been a huge tract of mobile homes, put there for the workers in several industries nearby. Not one family was left, though every sort and style and size of mobile home stood there.

He picked out a twelve-by-sixty, and I looked at it in dismay. "We'll never pull a really big one with this car, Amos."

"No sweat, Miss Luce. Now we know how to make somethin' to burn, we can use one of the big trucks. Better still, if you can drive one, you just take it on with you. Likely you'll need one sometime."

To one who began driving a Farmall tractor when she was three, too short to reach the brake so that my father set a bucket in the footrest plate for me to sit on, and I steered by reaching up above my head, this seemed like nothing much. With no traffic to contend with, I couldn't see too much that could go wrong, once I felt out the gears. I took it around the block two or three times, shifting up and down the range to get the feel. Then I backed up to the trailer again, missing it only twice. The third time I was right on the button.

Amos buckled up the hitch. Then we jacked up the supports, checked the tires for air, looked inside for personal things that should be left in town, on the remote chance that the owners might return and look for them. There wasn't a stitch of clothing, a spare toothbrush left. Only household items, sheets, cookware, and such, were left.

Suzi took the wheel of the Plymouth, and I set out for home, going extremely slowly until I was able to judge the length and breadth of my load accurately. But once we hit the highway I was able to let her out a bit. By mid-afternoon we were turning off the oil-top onto the long stretch of dirt road that wound past the Harkriders' and Mrs. Yunt's places.

We got home to find chaos compounded. As I swung cautiously into the curve that ended in our driveway, a slug glanced off my windshield, leaving a starred crack in its wake. I stuck my hand out the window and frantically signaled Suzi to stay where she was. I kept going, feeling like a juggernaut with my big tractor and huge load. Hunkering down until I could just see over the dash, I nosed the thing into the stretch of lawn that sloped downhill from the house to the creek.

A spatter of shot peppered the cab, but I kept on, seeing now a number of crouching shapes in the shrubbery on the downhill side of the house.

Zack's voice rang out, "Keep to the uphill side of the truck, Luce! The Ungers're down toward the creek!"

As I interposed the bulk of my vehicle between the house and its attackers, Zack, Lucas, and Elmond loped down to meet me. From their new vantage point they made it so hot for the attacking women that they hit for the river again, leaving one huddled shape among our japonicas. We waited for a while, to make certain that it wasn't a feint.

"What happened?" I asked Zack, as we peered from between the multiple wheels of the trailer.

"They hit the house. Thought, I suppose, that with the car gone and most of us in the fields they could wade in and loot the house without much opposition. Jim sent Sukie out the loft window into the chinaberry tree, and she scooted and got us. We've been keeping the heavy rifles in the field with us, just in case, and it was a good thing. Jim and Skinny held them off with the ten- and twelve-gauges, and Josh kept them from circling with the .22. He's a dead shot with that little popgun. When we got here they'd gone into a huddle down there in the bushes. We've been having spells of quiet and quick firefights since about two o'clock." He craned his neck, then stood and nodded.

"They're gone. I didn't think they had the intelligence to fake anything, but it's just as well to be sure."

Lucas hurried around the bend to wave the Plymouth on in, while the rest of us moved carefully toward the dreadfully still form on the ground where the wild violets always grew thickest in spring. She was older than the two I had seen when I shot the Unger. Maybe fifty, which would have made her one of the old woman's oldest daughters, I guessed. Like her mother, she was heavy and dirty, and under her grubby mackinaw she wore a red sweater. I had the uncanny feeling that it was the same sweater the Unger had worn when I shot her. She was as dead as they come.

By now there was a babble of talk as the children came from the house, the three women followed Lucas from the car, and Skinny and Josh hobbled out to see what was going on. One was missing, though. I rapidly tallied grownups and children, and suddenly I realized that Lisa was missing. With a word to Zack, I slipped away from the rest and went into the house.

She was crouched in a corner of the pantry that had been her bedroom until she was secure enough to join the rest of the young ones in the loft. Her hands were over her ears, and she was shaking so hard that her narrow bones seemed ready to clack together. When I lifted her, she shrieked, and her face screwed up into a mask of fear.

"Shhh, shh," I whispered, carrying her into the living room to the rocker. "It's all right, now. The shooting's stopped and nobody..." Then I thought. Somebody was killed. It might have been her mother or her grandmother who lay out there surrounded by enemies. "None of us are hurt," I finished after only a short pause.

She gave a shuddering sigh, and I felt her begin to relax against me. We sat there, slowly rocking, saying nothing, until the rest of the family came back. It was quite a long time, and I felt sure that Zack and Mom Allie, between them, had realized that the dead woman must be buried quickly and secretly, so that Lisa would never know. When Zack caught my eye and nodded, I knew that it had been done.

Now I missed another. "Where is Miss Vera?" I asked. She didn't answer our calls. She wasn't in the kitchen or the living room. But she was in the bigger bedroom, sitting in the small rocker there, a surprised expression on her face. Her heart, we surmised, had simply not been up to the stress of the day.

When Lisa saw her and realized that she was dead, she

did a very surprising thing. She walked quietly to the rocker, kissed Miss Vera on the cheek, and closed her eyes with one motion of her thin hand. It was a tender thing, lovingly done, and I wondered then and wonder still where she got the idea—or if, for once in her terrible childhood, she had seen someone among her own people do such a thing.

So we had exchanged one for one, but these were not pawns but living women. The reality of our situation came home to us with new clarity as we prepared Miss Vera for burial. We put her in my family's little plot beyond my old home place.

Sam was inconsolable. First the loss of his parents into the uncertain limbo of the blowup, then his great-grandmother's death seemed to shake the world beneath his small, square feet. Yet again, Lisa filled the gap. She took Sam into her lap in the big rocker, though he was hugely heavy for her, and she rocked him to sleep, though not one of us who were older had been able to manage it.

When all slept at last, I lay awake beside Zack listening to the night. Tomorrow, I well knew, would find us grappling with problems that we had hoped never to have to tackle.

CHAPTER TWELVE

There was only one bright spot in the next few days. Our four young newcomers to the family were well on their way to health again. Though they grieved loudly for their lost nurse, they continued to fill out and to thrive. So it was that when the first planting of corn was in the ground, we all pitched in to set the new "house" in place. The cabin seemed to be growing smaller by the moment.

It was a good time for digging. The wet winter had left the embankment soft enough for working, and we pitched into it and soon had a grave-like trough dug back into it. The trench was evened out to come just to the bottoms of the windows, and a slot was cut to give access to the door, once we had backed the thing into its permanent location. Then we proceeded to cover it over with the dirt we had removed, forming shored-up holes to the windows and adding a long vent pipe into the outside air for added ventilation. Onto one of these we attached a heat-grabber that slanted southward and that, with one of the pot-bellied stoves we had scrounged from town, was more than enough to keep it toasty on even the coldest days.

Suzi insisted on taking the job of "dorm mother." She had taken her turn, uncomplainingly, at everything we attempted, and we were glad to give her something to do that would absorb her time and attention to the exclusion of anything else. So one overcast day in late February, we had a housewarming for the new household in our growing commune. Lisa and Sam, La-Tonsha, Lillian, Jashie, Jim, Sukie, and Joseph crowded into the Burrow, as we had named the new house. Candy rode on Zack's shoulders, her head almost brushing the ceiling, and crowed with delight at everything.

The rest of us fitted in as best we could, admiring the three bedrooms, the two baths that were now connected into our water system and their own septic system, the built-in cabinets, closets, bookcases, and racks that made the most of the really large space that the place contained. One reason Amos had advised that we take this mobile was the fact that two of the bedrooms had three-tier bunk beds in them, the other containing a really vast king-sized bed. A very large family had evidently lived in it.

Our four "babies" were awestricken at the carpeting, the paneling, the prettiness of the new place, and it required no urging to get them to move into it with Candy and her mother. Even Joseph seemed to be quite content to remain there. To my astonishment, Jim and Sukie opted to join the new colony.

As I stood there, open-mouthed, Jim said, "Well, Mama, there are so many little ones. Suzi would be up and down all night long, taking them to the bathroom and giving them drinks of water. We're used to it now. You've no idea how many times we go up and down the ladder every night. We can each take charge of a room, and it'll work out fine."

I looked down at Lisa, who was by now scrooched up almost under my elbow. "Where do you want to live, Lisa?" I asked her.

She said nothing, but her big pale eyes pleaded. "You can stay in the cabin with us, if you'd like to," I answered her unspoken question. I could feel her relax.

Sam didn't wait to be asked. He dug in his heels, literally, hunched his square shoulders, drew in his chin that was already showing signs of its ultimate squareness, and said, "Want to stay at home."

We all nodded. Too many changes had already overtaken Sam. He and Lisa could share the loft, and Lisa could continue her healing role in his young life.

The first evening we all ate together in the cabin, all three households together. The shape of our future lives was coming together into a pattern, and for one evening we held onto the older way. Then we saw our eight pioneers to their quarters, going quietly and talking as we went. Before we reached the sunken doorway, Jim stopped.

"Listen!" he said.

We stood, ears cocked. Then we heard. Spring peepers were singing along the creek. The winter was all but behind us now. Zack put his arm around my shoulders and squeezed. I reached out to touch Jim and Sukie, growing now beyond my arm's reach. Far away a screech owl quavered, and another answered.

We saw the lights go on in the Burrow, and our two kissed us and went in. Lucas and his household said a soft good night and turned to go to their own rest. Only Nellie Sweetbrier stayed behind.

"Now that Vera's...gone, and the cabin isn't so crowded, could I stay with you?" she asked, her voice as timid as a child's.

Zack took her hand in his free one and said, "We'll be rattling around like dried-up acorns if you don't, Miss Nellie."

So now we picked up a different rhythm. Spring came with a rush, and we worked early and late in the fields and orchards and gardens. Mom Allie and Lantana set themselves the task of combing the burgeoning woods, finding and carefully transplanting the useful wild things that would stand being moved, and marking and staking patches of what we called the "immovables."

Suzi and I took on ourselves the chore of walking the fence lines, carrying shoulder packs filled with staples, claw hammers, wire cutters, and cans and buckets, together with trowels, for digging up anything that struck our fancies. In a way, that was the most pleasant job I ever found. For the most part the fences had survived the winter well. Only where they crossed washes and small creeks was there much repair work to do. Even with the heavy winds, not too many trees were down, and very few of those had struck fences in falling.

There was practical value in getting our fences into shape. Our herd, though small, was growing, and we intended rounding up strays to add to it. The woods, inside and outside our lines, were big and thick and full of bobcats, Southern red wolves, and occasionally cougars. Only if we kept our stock within our own range could we make certain none had wandered off or been killed.

The guns were a nuisance, but not one of us, no matter how young, went into the woods without one. We had made special trips to town after them, raiding private collections whose owners we had known. But as the weather warmed, the weight of all our gear, plus the shotguns, made us sweat. More than once, however, we glimpsed movement as we neared the fence lines that ran down toward the river, and we were more than glad to lug the extra weight.

As we neared the completion of our work, I became certain that we were under almost constant surveillance. We knew that we were watched, and we became adept at finding out our watchers, though they were too far away, always, for us to identify them by form or feature. By the time the work was done, I felt, uneasily, that we should question Lisa about the habits of her kin. That was a task I frankly declined, for she seemed to anchor her hold on a sane existence to Sukie and me, and I didn't want to send her back into the wordless state in which we had found her.

Nellie solved the problem for me. She was a wonder, Nellie Sweetbrier. At her age, which was almost sixty-five, and after the terrible injuries she had sustained, she would have been justified in taking only "easy duty." Instead, she reached out for everything she was physically able to do, and she must have peeled a mountain of potatoes, scrubbed acres of floors, washed numberless tubs of laundry that winter. Only in her sleep did the terrors of the recent past catch up to her, and more than once I woke to hear a stifled shriek, or a pitiful wail of "Jesse!" from Mom Allie's room, where she slept.

She had a sixth sense about what needed doing, so I shouldn't have been surprised, one March evening, when she looked across the supper table at Lisa and said, "Child, tell us about your family. You're bright as anything, and you've a good heart. Tell us what they did to make you like you were when we found you."

Two months ago it would have sent the child into a silent, white fit. A month ago it would have brought on a race to the pantry. Now she sat on the bench, watching the first early fireflies kindle their sparks across the patch of lawn and garden, and answered quite simply and calmly.

"They live down...down at the big water?" "Lake," I interjected, and she nodded and went on, "Men used to come to fish and drink and...do things with the big girls. They paid a lot of money, and Big Ma kept it in her own house. When we needed anything, she'd get Crazy Eddy to take the boat up to the other side of the...lake...and I guess he'd get a ride to town and bring back groceries and cloth and shiny things for the girls.

"Then one night there was a lot of rain and wind, and all the little dots of light we could see around the other edges of the water went out. They didn't come back on the next night, and the mail didn't come, either. The welfare checks were late, Big Ma said, and they never did come. We never went up the road farther than the first bend, before then. Big Ma didn't like cars. Even the men had to stop theirs down the road and walk up to the houses."

"You had several families there, then?" asked Zack with interest.

"No, not real families...not like this, just when one of the girls got so many kids that they made it too noisy for whatever house she lived in, Big Ma would make Crazy Eddy hire men to help him build another one. Just full of kids and girls. I guess there were"—she surreptitiously counted on her fingers—"four or five of them. Oh! One burned in the fall—somebody knocked a lamp over and the coal oil set the whole thing on fire. Got rid of a few of the noisy brats, Big Ma said."

We sat for a moment digesting this maternal reaction. Then Nellie said, "But someone must have taken care of you when you were little. Who was your mother? Did she take care of you?"

The pale Unger eyes were scornful. "Stinky Sarah used to say I belonged to her, when she needed to have something nasty done. It was Crazy Eddy I remember the most, though. He used to sneak me in something to eat when they locked me in the smokehouse and forgot about me. He'd sit there on the ground behind there and talk to me. Nobody else ever talked to me until I got here. I didn't know what he was saying, most of the time. Never knew words were anything but noise."

Now Nellie studied her carefully before asking her the next question. "When did they decide that something had really changed outside? What made them come up the river from the lake?"

Lisa thought a moment, her head down, hands still on the table. Then she said, "I guess it was the men—they stopped coming. No checks, and no mailman, and no suckers meant something was screwed up, Big Ma said. We ran out of canned stuff and light bread, and when Eddy went over to get some more he came right back. Nobody there, he said. Then Big Ma got the girls all together and picked out some of them to go scout out up the river. When they came back they said there were folks up there with good houses and plenty to eat, but they'd need me to weasel a way in. They didn't have guns, then. Just the pistol they gave me."

Zack nodded. "They probably got guns at Sim Jackman's. Harold said old Sim had a collection of every kind you can think of. They probably figured that the Jessups were armed, and it would be safer to trick them into opening up than to try to attack them." He turned to Nellie. "Were there any guns at your place? We didn't see any."

She nodded. "My little .22 and Jesse's twelve-gauge. They likely took them. They were in plain sight on the rack in the kitchen."

I reached over and took Lisa's hand. "They will come here again," I said, and I felt her muscles tense. "We'll have to fight them...maybe kill some of them. Unless you think it would do some good to try to talk to them?"

We watched with something like dread as she translated the words into whatever language she used interiorly, then looked up at me. "They kill people," she said, almost in a whisper.

"When they took me away, Eddy tried to make them leave me. They killed him with sticks." She shivered and looked away, and we shivered with her.

Then she looked, not at me or Nellie, not at Mom Allie or Sam, but straight into Zack's eyes and said, "They're bad. Kill them all!"

Disturbed, he nodded as if in agreement, and we all began to talk of other things, to stack the dishes for washing, to make cheerful and human sounds that would wash away from our inner eyes the terrible pictures the child's words had drawn for us. But I would guess that all did as I did and watched the dim line of woods by the creek from the corners of their eyes, seeing in the twilit depths movement that wasn't really there.

Still, we had learned something about the enemy. They were not only vicious and self-serving, they were not really quite human. In some way, the fact made the memory of those two still, red-sweatered bodies a bit easier to my conscience. In a world that seemed to be so suddenly depopulated, it seemed folly and worse for the few survivors to be slaughtering one another instead of putting our efforts together for our mutual survival.

When I said as much to Zack, he shook his head. "There've always been rogues, Luce. Remember in Houston...you never went out by yourself at night, because it simply wasn't safe. The streets were full of wild animals that walked on two legs but didn't have the faintest notion of how to be human. These are more of the same. I just wish to hell that Lisa had been old enough and understood enough to give us a good, sound notion of the way their minds work."

"Oh, I think I've a pretty good idea, I answered, swabbing out the sink and scalding the dishrag. "Anybody who could watch her grandchildren—or whatever they were—burn to death and just be glad to be rid of them doesn't have anything that you and I would recognize as a mind. We're going to have to have the same sort of caution the first settlers felt they had to acquire with the Indians. These savages are alien to us and our ways of doing things just as the Comanche were alien to the Spaniards. Total caution, taking no chances, shooting first to kill. That's got to be the name of the game from now on. And we don't take it for granted that they won't hurt the babies."

Zack muttered, and I realized with astonishment that he was cursing. Something he never does even under the most trying conditions. He was pale, and his eyes shone with unshed tears.

He turned his back and leaned his head against the cabinet door. I put my arms about him from behind and realized with pain that he was shaking with sobs.

Laying my cheek against his back, I held on for dear life, feeling the despair that racked him. I, too, had killed now. I thought I knew what was troubling him.

When he finally spoke, he said, "Luce, when I left 'Nam I swore that no matter what I'd never ever kill anybody again. No matter the things we did over there...the things the 'Cong did...I cut them out of my memory and swore never to put anything in their places.

"Now, here in my own place, with you and the kids and all these people we're responsible for, I've got to dig up those old corpses out of the past. I've got to remember how to scout for an ambush, how to watch for booby-traps, how to kill women and children.

"Oh, God, Luce! With all the filthy things blown to bits and a good crew pulling together down here in the woods—with food ready to jump out of the ground with the least encouragement...now we've got to pull out the blueprints and set up Hell again!"

CHAPTER THIRTEEN

Spring came on with fervor. Geese rose off the lake and came over us in honking skeins, heading north; the willows put on their new green; the treetops turned from gray to pink to lime-sherbet in a matter of days. The gardens were providing picked-off turnip green tops, tiny green onions, thumb-sized radishes, and delicately curled lettuce leaves, and we reveled in salads.

The seed potatoes and peanuts came out of storage, and we all sat down and cut seed potatoes and shelled peanuts for days at a time, for we intended to have a crop of spuds that would provide alcohol as well as food. Even the smallest were given a chance to help, though Joseph was limited to casting hailstorms of peanut hulls over all the activities when he tired of roaming about the yard at the end of his tether.

Life was a sleek stream of exhausting days and zonked-out nights while we got our crops into the ground. We even, thanks to Lantana, had sweet potato slips, for she remembered an old friend who always had them, no matter what.

Sure enough, we drove into Penrose, turned off onto a washed-out dirt road, and bounced along for what seemed miles, finally reaching a low brown house with a curl of smoke coming from the chimney. Aunt Sallie Zee had, as always, slips for sale, though she had no idea that she would have a customer this year. She was so glad to see us that she would have loaded us up with free plants and tubers and seeds, but we insisted on paying her in honey. We left her smiling and hugging the honey jar as if it were her only child.

When we got home, we went through the boxes and

bags and clumps of living stuff she had thrust upon us. Not only the regular things, but parsnip seed, spaghetti melon seed, early tomato plants, clumps of pansies, iris rhizomes, even a small woodbine curling up from its intricate root system. Wise Sallie Zee—she nourished our spirits, too. We planted and sorted and "toed in" and set out until we were all but permanently stooped.

But most welcome of all, she sent us a pair of puppies. We had been dogless for over a year, since our old Roger was killed by a snakebite. Now we were once again owned... and by the most fetching pair of part-German shepherd, part-husky pups I ever saw. They were just over two months old, sheer mischief covered with three-layered husky coats, and we all loved them instantly. And so did the goats. Punch and Judy, though so much taller, decided that they must be rather odd goats, and kept them busy when the children were worn out.

We debated long and hard over names. Then we named them Ted and Ginger, for no good reason except that they were names that would fit grown working dogs as well as they did pups. Their big paws and bright, quick eyes gave promise of future size and intelligence, and we knew that they and their offspring might well be the most valuable of our assets in days to come.

So far, our commune-like group had functioned well, though on an unorganized, catch-as-catch-can basis. The oldsters were too mature to engage in jealousy and squabbles, as younger people might have done—or some other old folks I could have named. Yet each of them had areas of unarguable expertise, which we valued highly and exercised to the greatest possible extent.

Even when Lucas began to come courting Mom Allie there was nothing but goodwill expressed. Though Zack and I were titular owners of the land we lived on, all of us knew that was past history. We worked with the others to decide on crops, division of labor, policies, and activities affecting all of us. So it was that we had formed, before we knew it, a working democracy on an ideally small scale, and even the children had a vote. Candy and Joseph being entirely too young to understand, we voted them by proxy until they were older; but even Jashie and Lillian, when things were explained to them very carefully, were thoughtful and intelligent when the time came to make their wishes known.

Not that we ever held "town meetings" before we acted. The way things came about, usually, there was no time for anything but roaring into action. Then, when there was time, we sat around and batted around our ideas on what might have been better to do. As we seemed to have nobody in the group who was the kind to sit and wring their hands, this worked ideally.

It was a good thing. One April morning we sent Jim and Sukie up the ridge to look for Hazel, the Jersey heifer, who had failed to come up to the barn the night before. We felt sure she was off with a new calf, and the children were wild to go.

It was still a strange feeling to check that both had shotguns and shells before sending them off. Still, I felt much more secure about them, knowing that both were well coached and practiced about using their weapons. I felt certain that no Unger, of whatever age, would be able to get within more than shouting range of the two, if that near.

We were now inundated with greens, beans, squash, cucumbers, and scads of other vegetables from the gardens, so I turned to with the pressure canner while Mom Allie and Lantana washed and peeled and shelled and sliced. Suzi was busy precooking those things that we preferred to can with their seasonings already cooked into them. So we were all busy as ticks in a tar bucket when there was a shrill whistle from the hill.

I looked up, a Klickit lid in my hand, to see Jim pelting down the slope with Sukie close behind him. There was no mistaking the urgency in them both, so I set the canner off the cook-stove, damped the fire, and wiped my hands dry as they drew near. When I turned to look, I found that the other women had done the same and were ready for whatever was to come.

They came panting up. Jim gulped, then said, "There's a big smoke downriver. It looks like it could be one of the houses. And it seemed like we could hear popping, maybe guns?"

I nodded. "Go get the men out of the field, Jim. Sukie, you get the little ones together and fort up in the cabin. Load all the guns and get the reloading equipment and check what cartridges need to be reloaded. Mom Allie, you want to stay and oversee them or go with us?"

My mother-in-law, who had always been in the van and forefront of everything going on, looked at me, then at Sukie. "I'll stay and help Sukie keep track of the young'uns," she said.

Meanwhile, Suzi had gone to the fence and whistled up the horses. Over the winter we had acquired mounts for all of us, and she saddled six of them (we stole the saddles, too), so that the men, when they came, wouldn't have to waste any time in coming after us. By the time we had rifles, ammunition, blankets, and first-aid gear ready, the horses were at the door.

We set out downriver at a good but not reckless pace. I rode ahead, as Zack had taught me, scouting out the country. My eyes were peeled for movement, for a dash of telltale red, for any sign of the presence of any of the Ungers. The woods were alive with woodpeckers and jays, with crows who commented rudely on our intrusion, but no human shape was visible anywhere. Behind me I could hear the reassuring thumps of the mounts that followed, so I upped the gait. It was much faster riding the overgrown track than it had been driving a mule and wagon over it, and sooner than seemed possible we reached the turnoff to the first farm.

I looked into the sky. Even above the trees smoke would have been visible if that had been the house that was burning. We trotted on without pausing. The Londowns' tract was next, and no smoke could be seen there, or at the Sweetbriers'. But I turned up the trail to Nellie's house, passed the silent structure, and from there we could see, bold against the spring sky, a boil of black smoke that must came from Bill Fancher's place.

We hit the road at a gallop, though I knew the horses were tired. By the road, it wasn't far to Bill's, though, and soon we reached the huge hickory tree that stood by the Fancher drive. We could hear gunfire clearly now, and I signaled a halt. We tied the horses in the shelter of the arm of woodland that divided Bill's cleared land from the road. Then we checked out the loads and slipped into the wood, deeper and deeper toward the house.

We spread out, Lantana on the left, Suzi in the middle, and I on the right. When I glimpsed a human shape ahead of me, I dropped to the ground and crawled to the big sweet-gum tree that halved the distance between us. Peering around, I could see an overalled figure lying on its belly, looking toward the house. As I watched, it raised a rifle and fired. I shot simultaneously, and the shape flopped once, then relaxed into the too-familiar look of death.

My "troops" were sound people. They didn't come running through the wood, crashing branches and calling out. I didn't hear a word from them, and I knew that they were going their own ways toward the house, and that anybody they met would rue the day.

The house, now that I could see it clearly, was ready to fall in. The heat from the blaze must have been ferocious, but a spatter of fire from the fencerow and the orchard told me that some, at least, of the family still held their ground. From a low shed on my right, I could hear a slow and deliberate marksman doing his best. I hoped it was Bill, and that none of his family had been killed. It seemed too much to hope, though, for I could hear gunshots of all gauges and calibers to right, left, and on the other side of the enclave.

A burst of gunfire sounded to my left. I heard the deep boom of Lantana's big old ten-gauge, from which she had removed the plug. One...two...three...four...five. That would be her full load. If there were many in front of her, she'd need cover while she reloaded. I ran, crouching, through the trees, calling to Suzi so she wouldn't mistake me for the enemy.

Lantana was flat behind a big post-oak stump, and slugs were whizzing about her position like angry bees. I circled toward the house until I could see her adversary, who was also dug in behind a sizable bole with a .22. There was so much noise, by now, that she didn't hear me until I was on top of her. When I nudged her with the barrel of my Springfield, she shrieked and dropped her light weapon.

This was one of the young ones. I was on the horns of a

dilemma, sure enough, now. I couldn't shoot her in cold blood. I wanted no adult Unger captives. Damn! I conked her with the butt and left her unconscious behind her tree.

Lantana poked her head over the stump. "Got her, Luce?"

"Got her. Come on, Auntie. It's getting too hot in there for the Fanchers. We've got to drive these critters off so they can move away from the house."

I turned and tripped over three bodies that had been hidden by a clump of saw vine. The evidence of the ten-gauge was staggering. I gulped down my last meal, which was threatening to rise up into daylight again, and we Injuned toward the house. On the way we eliminated one more Unger, a middle-aged harridan with a cast in her eye.

Suzi followed us from the shelter of the wood. We seemed to have cleaned out that side, so we ducked under the fencerow hedge and called softly, "Bill! Annie! Kids! Are you okay?"

A small voice said, "I am. Don't know about Papa, but Mama is in the shed with her rifle. The others are all over the garden and the orchard. It's hot!"

"Scoot to the shed and tell your mama to call everybody together. We've got 'em all out of the woods, and you can ease out over here. Then we'll take 'em from both sides. The men will be here pretty soon." I waited until I heard the crackle of footsteps through dead stalks.

Then I turned to Suzi. "Let me see," I said.

She drew a reddened left hand from behind her and held it nut. "How did you know?" she asked me, and I laughed.

"I've had too many cases when the kids wanted to hide cuts and bruises and burns that they got doing something they shouldn't. I can tell a mile off." I pulled the bandanna off my hair and made a fair job with it, leaving her thumb free, in case she needed to use the hand.

"You go back to the road. Zack'll come that way, through Nellie's. We think the same way, in a pinch, and I know it. Hurry them on. I'm going into the yard and help Annie get the children out...and find Bill." She took off as I scrambled through the wire, then picked a prickly way through the japonicas on the other side.

Annie was whistling the children into sight. Each child evidently had his or her own signal whistle, for as Annie trilled different patterns, she was answered from several quarters of the enclosed garden. Tony came first, sliding from the concealment of a grape arbor. He was followed, at intervals by four more of his siblings. Annie whistled again, two different trills.

There was no answer.

We looked at one another, and there was dread in her eyes. Then we marshaled the children into a line and sent them into the wood, one by one, as we watched for any activity that might show that the Ungers had filled up their depleted line on the road side of the house.

As the children disappeared into the trees, I heard a welcome sound. Hoof beats moved steadily toward us, not down the drive but through the arm of wood. As the last child darted for the cover of the trees, Zack came into sight, followed by Lucas and Josh.

The tight knot of apprehension that had lived under my collarbone dissolved. Now that Zack was here, things would be all right. So it had always been, all my life, and so it must be now.

Seeing my wave, he signaled back. They would ride around the fencerow and take the besiegers on the other sides by surprise. Annie caught my elbow and raised her eyebrows. Somehow, in these circumstances, words weren't really necessary. I nodded, and we turned back into the now-blistering garden to look for the missing.

We found Bill slumped against a peach tree, a crimson groove along his skull bleeding freely. He was out, so we put a pressure bandage over the wound, tying it tightly with a strip of Annie's shirttail. A small girl was crumpled ominously under a frame full of berry vines.

Annie moved her gently, feeling for a heartbeat. I could tell that she had found one by the sudden relaxation of her tense back.

Phyllis, this child, had a broken shoulder. The slug had shattered bones and torn muscles. She was bleeding badly, and it was impossible to see how to stop it, placed as we were. As we stooped there, Suzi came softly up behind us and looked the situation over.

"You put her on my shoulder," she said quietly. "I'll carry her to Jessups', down the road. Then you come, when all is done." Suzi was small, but so was Phyllis, so we lifted her carefully onto the slender shoulder, packing the wound with the rest of Annie's shirt and part of mine. She set off sturdily, and I smiled at Annie with all the reassurance I could find.

The third child, Ron, was hard to find. We finally crawled through the orchard, searching every inch of the ground. He was buried under a heavy-leaved branch from a plum tree that had been literally cut off its mooring by gunfire. Somewhere out there one of those creatures must have had an automatic weapon, pilfered from the Army.

Ron was unwounded except for a knot on his head where the branch had struck him. We tugged him back to the shelter of the thick fencerow hedge before examining him thoroughly, and by then the sporadic fire had died away entirely. We laid him beside his father, and Annie sat beside them while I crept to the yard gate to reconnoiter.

Our three cavalrymen were sitting their horses in a line, watching something toward the river woods. I gathered that our enemies were in full retreat, so I hailed them.

"We need to get Bill down to Jessups'. He's hurt. Suzi is carrying one of the other children down there too. Is it safe to move from here?"

Lucas raised his hand, then rode slowly toward the river, his gun across the pommel of his saddle. Zack and Josh trotted toward me, and Zack called out, "They're going toward the river. I think they've had enough for now. Lucas is just seeing that they keep going."

He dismounted and gave me a quick hug as he entered the gate. Josh, just behind him, grinned. But they both got busy when they saw Bill's gray face.

By the time Lucas returned from his patrol, we had Bill and Ron loaded onto one of the horses. We went up the drive to find the other three still safely tethered. It was a relief to mount again and move away from the burning house and kindling fruit trees into the smoke-free air of spring. Yet I caught Annie looking back toward the column of black with regret on her face.

"We worked so hard...we had to fight so hard to keep it. Now it's gone. What'll we do, Luce?"

My mind went into gear. "There's a house, empty, just upriver, not a half mile from us. I don't know whose it was, but it's tight and whole. We can always scrounge anything you need, and your cattle are safe. I saw them all bunched in a thicket as we came down through the woods. You'll be all right. We're going to be a colony, now, not just chance neighbors."

CHAPTER FOURTEEN

We caught up with Suzi on the way. She had had to stop and lean against a tree, but she hadn't dared to put Phyllis down, for fear of causing even more bleeding. Zack had them both in hand before Suzi really knew we were there. He put her up on his horse, then walked beside her, carrying the child. Suzi swayed in the saddle, her olive face paled to paper whiteness

"Arm...hurts," she said, as he led her mount down the Jessups' drive.

I nodded and looked back at Zack. He jerked his chin, and I galloped ahead to warn the Jessups of our coming. They were both on the patio, watching the boil of smoke from the Fanchers' house. Horace greeted me with a booming cry of, "We just now spotted the smoke, or we'd have been over! What happened? More Ungers?"

"More Ungers," I agreed, dismounting and slipping the bit so that the gray could graze. "We saw the smoke before noon, and Lantana and Suzi and I came running while Jim went for the men. There must have been a bunch of 'em around the house...I never saw any except for those on the upper side of the house, but it sounded like a war while the men were rousting them out of the bushes toward the river. Anyway, Bill's hurt...scalp wound. Lost a lot of blood." I paused.

"The little girl, Phyllis, is badly hurt. Chest and shoulder wound. We didn't have a chance to explore it, but I think she's still bleeding. One of the boys got knocked out by a falling branch, but I don't think he's much to worry about."

Carrie glanced sharply at the approaching cavalcade,

then she turned toward the house. Her call brought both her daughters flying from the rear garden, and I was relieved to see that Grace seemed to have recovered well from her wound. Laura, however, still wore a strained look, and she was far too thin.

Then Sim Jackman came hobbling from the kitchen door, and I gazed at him open-mouthed. He looked, as indeed he was, if he had been broken all to pieces and put back together with glue by an inexperienced hand. He moved stoutly, for all that, and had us all hustling wood for hot water, blankets, and alcohol for the wounded before we could say hello.

Horace and Josh bore Bill into the flagged kitchen. He was beginning to come around, though he was still a frightening shade of ashen gray. As soon as his eyes opened they glanced wildly about for his family, and Annie laid her hand on his shoulder.

"All here, honey," she said. "None dead."

Then he lay back and let Lantana and Carrie work loose the makeshift bandage in order to clean his wound. They carefully kept him turned so he couldn't see Phyllis, who had been placed on the dining table.

Sim and I bent over her and I cut away her coveralls and shirt. There was no need to loosen dried blood—it hadn't dried and was still oozing slowly from the ugly spot in her shoulder.

"Had much 'sperience with gunshot wounds?" the old man asked, as I straightened my back and laid the scissors aside.

"Not much," I answered. "This is way beyond me, Sim. We need a doctor, I'm afraid."

"I been tendin' to hunters that shot each other accidental for over thirty years," he told me. He lifted an Xacto knife and a large pair of tweezers from the pan in which we had boiled them and leaned over the child again. "They made pure D messes out of each other, sho 'nuff. I've seen worse 'uns than this, by a long shot."

But I could tell from the set of his jaw that digging slugs out of a seasoned hunter was a far different thing from the task now before him. Phyllis's golden-tawny skin had a bluish undertone, and her breath came in shallow gasps.

"Ain't an artery," Sim muttered. "Wouldn't be here now if it was. Just a really nasty mess down there. Pieces of bone all in it. Kin you see to pick out some of it on your side, while I try for the slug?"

I plied my tweezers and held my hand steady and my mind detached. One day I might well have to do the same for one of my own children, and I intended to know the right way to go about it. We were working so closely that I could follow the motions of his knife and his pincers without neglecting my own task.

The bone shards gleamed in the light of the lamps that Carrie had set in their hoops in the chandelier overhead. The blood was redder than natural, the instruments brighter. Still, I picked out fragments and watched the misshapen chunk of lead emerge from the tender flesh and clink into the pan that Zack held. Then floods of alcohol—made by the directions we had left with Horace—cleaned the hole, and what seemed to be yards of damp cotton went into it.

"Soaked them bandages in comfrey tea," said Lantana behind me. "Mighty good for healing."

She pushed me aside, then Sim, and took over the final bandaging, wrapping wide strips of what I knew must be an irreplaceable sheet about chest and shoulder and neck, until Phyllis couldn't possibly move about enough to rip anything open. Then we laid the child back and watched, breathless, for a long time. No blood came through, then or later.

Annie, with iron control, had stood back and let us take her child into our less-than-expert hands and work for her life. Now she folded quietly into a rocking chair, her face as ashy as her husband's had been. Carrie and Lantana zipped into action, and soon we each held a cup of mint tea well laced with "drinking alcohol."

By now Bill had come around, though he was—and would be—pretty wobbly. There was no way to hide from him the serious condition in which Phyllis now existed, but he took it well. There's no denying that our fortifying tea helped in that respect, and not only Bill.

We were all shaken and sick. The menace of the Unger community, that we had buried away from our thoughts with work, now stared us directly in the eyes. Something must be done. Once we had the Fanchers settled wherever they decided to go; once we had reinforced the Jessups as much as could be done; once we barricaded our own complex of homes so that no other sneak attack could catch us unaware; then we must go on the offensive ourselves.

It was now mid-afternoon. The weather, which had been almost hot, as April is in East Texas, now held the muggy feel that precedes a thunderstorm. We knew that some of us, at least, must return home to reassure those left behind, as well as to reinforce them in case the Ungers tried another foray.

Lantana elected to stay for a while and help care for the wounded, a choice much appreciated by Carrie Jessup. Suzi wanted nothing except to go home to her brood of children.

Josh and Horace felt that his added rifle would make enough to hold the Jessups' house if new trouble should arise. So four of us mounted the horses and moved off into the now-cloudy afternoon, though my own thoughts kept wandering back to the eight-year-old who still lay within the grasp of death.

As we turned down the Sweetbriers' drive, Lucas cleared his throat, a sure sign that he was preparing to impart an idea. "You know, it's dangerous business going into those woods down by the river, with the Ungers licking their wounds. 'Round by the road is ridiculous. But if we cut straight through the fields and pastures behind all these places, we'd make it a lot straighter way, with no woods for anybody to set up an ambush in. Have to cut a lot of fences, but that's just good for the cattle, except just Fanchers' and Londowns' spreads. We can put in gaps there, that we can close behind us."

It was so obvious—and so bright—that it had escaped us all until now, So we painfully cut barbed wire with pliers, as we had no wire cutters handy, making a straight shoot toward our own farm. At Bill's first fence we carefully parted the wire, tied onto the loose ends a stout hickory sapling, made two loops of wire that we had saved when coming through non-strategic fences, and closed it by setting either end of the pole into a loop, which was no easy task, and left the fence nicely tight.

"Have to bring some staples to reinforce the wire on both posts," Zack decided. "But we can do that when we come back after Lantana."

The new route, even with the delays involved, got us home before sundown. Not a sign of anything hostile could be seen the whole way, and we found things quiet, though alert, at home.

Amazingly, Nellie, the children, and Mom Allie had finished the canning, short-handed though they were. This was a blessing, for we knew that the next day must be spent in fortifying our enclave. There was no longer any way we could avoid facing the necessity. It must be done, and now, lest we find ourselves in such a fix as the Fanchers had faced.

We rose before sunrise, all three households. Suzi, though in pain, would not be left out, so we set her to weaving leather lattices to hang inside the windows. Not only would they catch shattered glass, but we also hoped that they would make it harder to see anyone moving in the house. With summer upon us, it would be impossible to stay in the houses with the shutters closed.

The rest of us set our minds to those selfsame shutters. Our cabin was fitted with stout ones, into which we now bored loopholes. The other house was also supplied with shutters with loopholes. We blessed our tin roofs, for it was upon the Fanchers' shingled one that the Ungers' flung torch had started the fire that destroyed their home. In order to give even more protection from fire, we banked dirt up the walls of both houses, almost to the overhang of the roof. Maud found herself harnessed to the slip, dragging big scoops of soil up from the near field for us to shovel against the logs.

So desperately did we work that in two days both freestanding houses were clad in earthworks. We also set heavy stakes into the tunnels that led to the windows of the ex-mobile home that now housed the children. Slanting them outward so that their sharpened ends loomed dangerously in the dimness, we found ourselves nodding with satisfaction. Fire or bullet could not, we felt, find a way to the little ones.

Now we dug into our scrounged arsenal and cleaned and loaded shotguns and rifles to keep in handy spots in all three places. With so many young children about, this was nervous work. In order to give them a true idea of the danger of the weapons, we took everyone over three out into the creek meadow and gave them shooting lessons. The blast of noise, plus the vicious kick, made them all cautious and respectful of the guns that lived in their homes with them. The very youngest were held in arms near enough so that they got the full effect of the shots. We could only hope that they would remember.

When we felt that we were reasonably secure, we knew it was time to check on the refugees at the Jessups'. We were not easy in our minds about having our only neighbors so distant from us. In case of another attack, only chance could warn those who were not directly involved.

On the third morning after the one whose work had been so violently interrupted, we set out again. Mom Allie elected to join Zack and me, leaving Elmond to oversee a new attack on the overflowing gardens. We seemed, as I looked along the line of horses (we had two pack animals with us, just in case they might be needed), like nothing so much as a gang of bandits from a Western movie. Our clothing had suffered; our skin was rough and browned from our long hours in the fields. All in all, we looked as mean and lowdown as the Ungers.

We went across fields, following our line of cut fences. As we came up behind that first farm that we had found untenanted on our initial foray downriver, we moved near, dismounted, and checked on the condition of the house.

The back door had locked itself when we closed it before. A bit of work with one of Mom Allie's huge wire hairpins had it open in a moment. The stink of mildew was horrible, and we set doors and windows wide to the April sun. If the Fanchers decided to settle here, we would have an all-hands-to cleaning bee, I decided. Aside from the smell, the house was nice. Big rooms, six of them, plus a sun porch across the back where pots of blackened stubble told of the deaths of many pot plants.

There was a fireplace in the den. Its chimney backed

against the interior wall, and it was even pierced for a flue, though the opening was covered with one of those metal "pie plates" with a country scene pasted onto it...ideal for setting in a wood cook-stove. The high ceilings showed no leak spots. With a bit of earth-moving work, the place could be made pretty defensible, Zack felt certain.

Outdoors, we could see that someone had taken great pains with the place. There were several fruit trees, a grape arbor, and the traces of a big garden, where volunteer okra and cherry tomatoes and mustard were already growing in haphazard clumps. Evidently the soil was well conditioned and fertile. We left the house open, wondering why the Ungers hadn't bothered to raid it. Locking it would have invited a broken door, if they returned. Perhaps it had been just too much trouble for their unstable minds to bother with.

We moved on across the fields, and as we approached the Londowns' land we saw Curt and the boy looking at our makeshift gap in the fence. We hailed them before they saw us, for both carried rifles.

"We brought some staples to make that tighter," Zack called, as we rode up. "It's too dangerous to ride the river anymore. Did you know the Ungers attacked and burned out the Fanchers, down your road?"

Curt shook his head. His mouth was tight, and his eyes didn't look at all friendly.

"We're going to check on the family right now," I said. "We helped them fight off those women, then we took them to Jessups'. Bill and his little girl were badly wounded. We left some of our people there to help stand guard. If we all work together maybe we can get those Unger women under some kind of control—or kill them."

He spoke for the first time. "The Fanchers—niggers, aren't they?"

I looked at him in shock. Even before the blowup, that sort of talk had been dying away among all except a few die-hards. Now that there were so few of us, color didn't enter into our calculations.

Zack's voice was hard as he said, "They're good, stout, clever people. Good at fighting off Ungers. Good at surviving. Good with their hands and their heads. If they'll come, we're going to move them into the house nearest us. That way we can be of some help to each other without having to fight through Ungers to get back and forth."

Londown grunted, his gray eyes as expressionless as such eyes can be. Then he said, "Don't fancy gettin' cozy with no niggers. Might not mind you all, but not them. We've done all right, just keepin' to ourselves, anyway. "

Zack was a bit flushed, but his voice was calm. "If that's the way you want it, okay, but some morning if you wake up with your roof on fire from one of those she-devils' torches, just let off some shots. We'll probably come and bail you out. Black ones and all."

He touched his heels into Coalie's flanks, and as I turned Friz to follow him, I was watching Londown's face. It had the turtleish expression of one who knows his kind is extinct but absolutely refuses to admit it to himself. Times had changed out of all recognition. Unless Curt Londown managed to change a bit to suit, I suspected that he might well go down, taking his family with him.

CHAPTER FIFTEEN

With so many hands at work, it didn't really take long to get the Fanchers settled into their new home. Though the Jessups had offered to move them all into their capacious stone fortress, Bill and Annie had decided that so many children injected into an all-adult household might make problems for everyone. I felt certain that Carrie had breathed a silent sigh of relief, though her invitation had been heartfelt. She was not young, and I could tell, in my short visits with her, that noise tore up her nerves.

She and Horace supplied many items that were needed. They had spent their lives wandering, but when they finally sent down roots they collected things at an amazing rate. The blowup had found them equipped with a little bit of almost everything.

The storage shed at Fanchers' had survived the fire, and there Bill had stashed the "finds" he had made at Sim Jackman's. A bowlegged wood cook-stove was the most valuable of these, but blacksmithing tools, chisels, punches, bits, leather-working tools, and many more items came out of that storeroom, and we rejoiced to see them.

Once we had the house earth-banked and the roof sheathed with tin we scrounged from several old hay sheds, they insisted that we return to our own burgeoning crops and let them cope. This we did, after helping them drive their cattle down the road and into the new pastures. We rather regretted cutting the fences so thoroughly before we were through mending them.

By now we were well into May, and we turned the children out with buckets, baskets, boxes, and hats to pick dewberries by the bushel. With our plentiful supply of honey (which also helped in making our alcohol) we jellied and preserved and "jammed" until all four households bulged with sweet stuff. And no sooner had the berries slacked off than the plums, both wild and tame, came on.

By June we had exhausted the bulk of the garden stuff, drying much of it, though we had rigged Savoniuses for the other families and scrounged freezers for them, too. Still we felt that it was better to start in the way we must go. Freezers, we knew, once worn out could not be replaced.

The first really hot days found us with a brief breathing spell while we waited for the hay to reach its full growth. For the first time in months we took thought to the children's education

Annie, we found, was far ahead of us.

"The way I see it," she said in her carefully precise English, "is this. The things schools taught before are mostly useless now. Who needs to know bookkeeping—or will for generations? Nobody has use for civics, for instance. Civics is as dead as the dodo. What our young ones need is to read, to write a clean hand, to be able to use math, geometry, and logic. Most of the rest they'll get by reading. In your books you have something on everything I ever heard of, and they can get their history and geography and philosophy from reading them.

"Among us we can find somebody who knows quite a bit about a lot of things. The children will learn from us while they help us do what we know how to. But for learning to read, write, and do simple math, they can teach each other much better than we can. Mine have been doing that since the blowup. Those who can read teach those who can't. As the five-year-old learns, she teaches the three-year-old. My two-year-old can read simple things like *Hop on Pop* right now."

"But will they?" Mom Allie asked, interestedly. "How do you make 'em accept the responsibility?"

"By not letting them know it's a responsibility," Annie replied. "They do it for fun. Getting down the books is the biggest thrill they can think of, and if they're bad they don't get to study. Kids like to learn. It's only schools and sorry teachers that have made them think it's miserable hard work."

I nodded with agreement. "Remember last winter, Mom Allie? Jim and Sukie started out hating the thought of having to do schoolwork. But with no TV, no school itself, no outside people or ideas, before Christmas they were diving into it every evening, without being told. I hadn't really thought about it, what with everything, but it's been working right here. Do you know that Candy can say her ABCs? And count? And recognize both letters and numbers? I'll bet you anything that the other under-fives are learning, too."

And they were. When we checked (very cautiously), we found that Suzi was taking home armloads of books from the cabin every day or two. Jim, when asked very offhandedly, said, "We have a ball, Mom. The little ones want to know everything and why it's so, and it keeps Sukie and me busy reading up, every night, so we can answer their questions."

"Do you think they might like to learn something new—say, Spanish?" I asked innocently. "I found my old records from the course I took, and we could rig a phonograph over there, if you wanted."

"That'd be neat!" he breathed. "We could play with it every night."

So our educational processes went on with even more verve than our agricultural ones, though many evenings all the young ones were too tuckered to do anything but lie in the fragrant summer grass and play word games or practice their Spanish. Even Lisa, whose life had not included even the concept of schooling, took to the books and the new ideas with relish. By midsummer, we were astounded at the amount we all had learned, for we soon found that an hour spent batting words and facts and strange philosophies around the bunch of us not only rested our bodies but kept our minds from going stale.

The first of the hay was cut and stacked, according to Lucas's remembered formula. The stacks stood along the edges of the hayfields like African huts, and each forkful had been laid neatly arranged around the central poles so that the rains of the winter wouldn't run into the stack. New hay was beginning to get deep in the fields when we began picking the corn that had dried on the stalks. We filled every bin and crib and shed that could be made weatherproof and (we hoped) rodent-tight. This would be the basis for our alcohol for the next year, and the protein-rich residue would feed all our cattle.

We had washed up, one scorching July evening, and were waiting for Nellie, Suzi, and Lisa to finish getting supper on the table when a familiar yet alien sound reached us. Zack stood up in one motion and reached for his rifle. I followed suit, as did the rest of our crew. Skinny and Josh melted into the shrubbery, and the children scooted for their burrow. Mom Allie and Lantana made for the cabin and took up their posts.

So it was that when a four-wheel-drive pickup jounced into view, only Zack and I stood waiting for it to come to a stop. We didn't exactly hold our rifles on it as the driver got out, but it wouldn't have taken a second to have him in our sights.

He was a surprise. In his neat Highway Patrol uniform, he might have stepped, entire, out of the lost past. However, he had his handgun out, and his expression was not really reassuring.

He waved the thing at us, motioning us back.

Obligingly, we stepped one pace backward.

"Harley Schmidt," he grunted.

"*Gesundheit*," I replied, gravely, and Zack snorted with laughter.

"This is no game, ma'am," he said sternly, waving the pistol again. "I'm the only government this whole area has left, from Dallas to the Coast. It's my job to see everybody knows the rules and lives by 'em. I've got the Texas Criminal Code in the truck, plenty of copies for everybody. Anybody doesn't take 'em serious, I'll have to take 'em in."

"To where?" came Lantana's voice from the cabin. "You goin' to jail everybody who spits on a sidewalk? Go along, man. There's no more government, far as we are concerned. Just little dabs of folks like us who are too busy surviving to worry about a lot of foolishness."

Schmidt's face grew pink. "Respect for the law..." he began, but Zack finished the sentence: "... is as dead as the dodo. Like civics. Like bookkeeping. Like income taxes and dope peddling and graft and meddling government agencies. Like State Highway Patrolmen. You must give yourself tickets. There's nobody else on the roads we've seen.

"People need somebody to take care of 'em," Schmidt yelled.

"Go tell that to the Ungers. We've been doing fine taking care of ourselves. They've been doing their best to take care of themselves, robbing and killing what few people they can find. If you really want to do something useful, warn anybody whose road ends at the lake or the river that those critters are loose and armed. Better yet, get some of 'em together and bring 'em here and we'll all go down together to the lake and finish off the whole mess."

"Or you can take them off to jail," I added sweetly to Zack's statement.

Schmidt's face grew even pinker. "Folks like you're the very ones got this country in the fix it's in," he grunted. "Takin' the Law for somethin' to laugh at. Coddlin' pinkos and pansies and niggers. I'm not lettin' you get away with it. I've got me an organization started, and we're goin' to clean up this end of the state. Maybe the rest of the country's gone, but we're goin' to have law and order right here."

"You poor goop," said Zack patiently. "Can't you see that even if you had a thousand nuts like yourself you couldn't get things back like they were? People just don't have time to play games any more. We're busy, every day of every week of every month, just making sure that we and our family can survive for the next day and week and month. You try to take up our time with permits and such, and we'll not stand for it."

"Besides," I added, "I can't see even you running around the roads trying to put Humpty-Dumpty back together again and letting your people go hungry. So I gather that you're a bachelor with no family. But anybody who has people who depend on him isn't going to bother with you, whether he agrees with you or not."

From the frown that crossed his face, I decided that I was at least partly right. That didn't prevent him from making another reckless gesture with his handgun.

Evidently Mom Allie had had enough. A slug thunked into the ground beside his polished boots, and she said, "Drop that thing, sonny, before you hurt somebody."

He dropped it. I would have, too, for she used the voice a good mother uses just before she unlimbers the peach tree switch.

Zack bent over and picked it up, jacked the cartridges out. Then he tossed the gun back to Schmidt. "Put that away. Maybe you can talk sense without having it in your hand."

A bit of the stuffing seemed to disappear with the weapon, for he didn't know what to do with his hands as he listened to my husband put our position into the simplest English he could manage.

"We are surviving. We are taking in anyone who is willing to work with us. We have hurt only those people who have tried kill us. We will not take any guff off a tin-pot clunk that nobody needs anymore. You come back, alone or in company, with the idea of arresting us or making us toe your imaginary mark, I will send you back with lead in your pants. I hereby declare this the United Area of Hickory Hollow, free and independent of any body or governmental entity that went before. We have one code: work for the common good or get out, alive or dead, as you prefer."

I put my arm around him and gave him a hug.

Schmidt glared at us for a moment, got in his truck, and backed out around the curve of the drive. We could hear him gunning his engine all the way up the road and out of earshot.

"If we're lucky, he'll run out of gas before he can get back around to us," Zack sighed. "But isn't it strange how some people just can't accept the fact that things have changed?"

Mom Allie came out of the cabin wiping her hands on her apron. "We'll have to keep an eye out for him, now, just as we do the Ungers. That's the kind that can't take the idea that he has lost his clout. I've met a thousand of him along the way. They're worse than the seven-year itch. Can't seem to get rid of 'em."

Lantana, following her, nodded. "Might be," she said worriedly, "we ought to warn 'em downriver, just in case he works the other road. Way he talked, the Fanchers might have trouble with him."

We looked at one another. We had worked without letup in the fields and the gardens. It was too early for planting the fall gardens, the hay was coming on, the corn gathered and its stalks also chopped and fermenting in our alcohol vats. We needed...really needed...a holiday.

The whole crew was at supper at the long table under the sweetgum tree in the back yard of the cabin. We had found that cooking two meals was a waste of manpower, so we combined forces during peak working seasons. When we broached the subject of a combined day off and picnic down the river, they were fired with enthusiasm.

"But can we risk leavin' the places empty?" Lucas asked at last. "Seems pretty dangerous."

"I think I can solve that," Zack answered. "My job in 'Nam was booby traps. And if you can undo them, you can, by golly, do them. Though I hate the thought of it."

So it was that the next morning was spent in sandwich-making (we had figured a way to make sourdough bread using a mix of cornmeal and ground oats that would hang together pretty well) and in booby-trapping buildings. Zack, with his usual long-range vision, took all the children with him to "help." They would always know where the traps were and what they looked like, as a consequence. And after he "blew" one for their edification, they were unwilling to get too near any of the locations. Children, contrary to the views of our late culture, are not fools.

By ten o'clock we were ready. Most of us elected to walk. Some rode horses. The older folk preferred to ride in the wagon. We looked like the Westward Migration when started off through the cut-fence road.

Our first stop at the Fanchers' was welcomed enthusiastically. We found the family gathered about a sick cow. Mom Allie and Lucas diagnosed her problem as bloat and Lucas inserted the small blade of his pocket-knife into the barrel of her belly just before the hip. A rush of foul gas sent us all retreating into shade of the yard.

The Fanchers were as ready for a holiday as we were. In a fast scramble, they got food together, set their standing traps and trip ropes against intruders, and were ready to join us. So we set out again across the pastures.

At the Londowns' fence we paused to send Zack to the house. We crossed the "hostile territory" and waited for him beyond the fence that bounded his land on its other side. It wasn't long before Zack came pelting back, and I could tell the way he sat his horse that he was mad clean through.

Though he said nothing to the others, he hitched his horse to the tail of the wagon and walked beside me for a while. When we were far enough behind the others, he said very softly, "That bastard Curt is enough to make you sick. He never thanked me for warning him about Schmidt...said he sounded like the sort of man who ought to take things in hand now. 'We need a strong hand,' he told me. Strong hand! What those two want is a penny-ante dictatorship set up in the place of the state that's gone. With themselves in the driver's seat, of course. Wouldn't surprise me if that fool went galloping off to join Schmidt and left his family to take care of themselves."

I could feel him seething beside me as we walked, so I said, "Why don't we have Bill keep a very distant eye on their place and warn us if Curt leaves for any length of time? The Ungers would be on them fast, if they knew he was gone. Cheri and the two older children just haven't enough numbers to hold them off."

He grunted agreement. And we walked in silence for a time in the blaze of the July morning. A hawk circled high, and two buzzards moved even higher as barely discernible specks. A coachwhip snake went shooting through the grass beside us, and crackles of grasshoppers fanned up in front as we wandered across the deep-grown grass.

From the wagon, Nellie called, "Could we go by the house? I'd like...I'd like to put some greenery on Jess's grave." We turned toward the distant roof, but the track we had followed in the winter was now lost in the rampant growth of grass and hushes. The yard, too, was lost in weeds and grass. But in the orchard small sweet peaches hung on the trees.

"We'll get a load of these when we come back," Nellie said. "I know how to dry them...Mother used to do that."

There was deep shade about Jess Sweetbrier's resting place, and we sat there while Nellie found ferns and planted them about the now-sunken grave. Then we moved into the orchard again to eat our lunch, finishing it off with peaches in disgraceful amounts.

After a short rest, we moved away again, and I saw that Nellie didn't look back even once. I nodded to myself, and Zack, always on top of everything, took my hand.

"We're all of us through with looking back," he said. "Forward is going to be all anybody can handle for quite a while."

CHAPTER SIXTEEN

Our short day of outing was over too soon, but it renewed the ties we felt with those down the way. The Jessups were faring well, though Sim had never fully regained his strength. All of them came with us a bit of the way, when the lowering sun told us it was time to start homeward.

Zack and I, walking at the rear of the big group of people, felt like the founders of some new tribe. Carrie and Horace, walking with us, voiced our feelings well when Horace said, "You know, it seems odd to us older ones, but this is the way it's going to be, from now on. Groups like this, every kind of people from all kinds of backgrounds, working together."

"Like a family," Carrie chimed in. "Fighting like crazy, sometimes. Having all sorts of fits and fallings-out. But still standing up for one another when things get tight.

"You know, we intend to go over, when we've the time, and pull things together at the Sweetbrier place. We feel as if, with all these young ones, in a few years there'll be new families to need houses. It'd be a shame to let good houses fall down from lack of care, when they'll be needed."

"Now who's looking ahead?" I teased her. "I hadn't thought that far, myself, but you're right. We could make this whole five miles of river land one community. Except for the Londowns, of course."

She frowned, but Horace boomed, "Sounds as if Londown and Schmidt would make a good team. Hang on to old prejudices and worn-out rules and useless things like that until you manage to put the rest of us under, that's the motto of that kind. I suppose they just can't let themselves realize that the old world is gone as thoroughly as ancient Greece."

Zack sighed. "Some people—a lot of them—really hadn't any inside security. Just artificial things like authority or feeling superior because of their color or politics or such-like gave them their self-esteem. And now we have to cope with surviving, with Ungers and their kind, and with witless wonders like those, too. What a pain!"

Nevertheless, the reminder of Harley Schmidt cast a pall over our good-byes. It wasn't leavened much by Horace's parting gift. He had carried a long, oddly shaped parcel all the way, and as we reached the first fence line he thrust it into Zack's hands. "Here. Try it out. When you get home, let 'er rip for a few blasts. If we can hear you, then we'll know you can hear us, if anything comes unglued."

It was a battered trumpet. Zack raised it to his lips and emitted a wild squawk, but Horace stood there in the hot summer afternoon and gave him a short lesson in getting the most sound possible from the thing. And when Zack raised a respectable blast, Horace grinned. "Got one like it," he said. "Just say if either end of the line hears a hoot, it's a sign of trouble. If, that is, it can be heard. I'll answer you, if I hear you, and we'll all be listening, in about an hour or so."

The young ones could hardly wait to get home and try out the new system, so we made good time across the grown-over fields and pastures. As we crossed Londowns', we could see the whole family lined up before their garden fence, watching us. There was no wave, no hail, nothing. It seemed such a pity, with so few of us left, that his children should be so isolated, but I suppose he thought our dark-complexioned children had already contaminated our lighter ones and would also spread some sort of plague to his own.

The shadows were long before we reached our own lane. Lucas and Elmond slipped ahead of the bunch to reconnoiter, and we followed slowly, quietly, waiting for their signal. The birds were celebrating the first coolness of evening with many-voiced enthusiasm. Along the creek beside us the frogs had tuned up, trebles first, then mid-tones, and lastly the true bassos. It was a moment so lovely, so fragile, that I held my breath, fearing that our scouts might find something terribly amiss to spoil it. But Lucas's clear old voice called, "All's fine and dandy," and we came up the lane under a crimson-streaked sky.

At the gate Zack lifted the horn and blew, once, twice, three times, shocking the birds to silence. Then we waited. After a little, we could hear, faintly but clearly, the trumpeted reply. A communal sigh told me that all of us had held our breaths, waiting.

Lantana turned her lined face up to the sky. "Good thing we went now," she mused. "Weather comin'. Tomorrow, next day, weather comin' for sure."

Which meant that we rose the next morning and hastily saw to the security of our haystacks, our corn bins, and our stills. Suzi and I turned under the dried bean vines in the garden and planted fresh greens, beans, and squash, while the others scattered to their own tasks. When the lunch call was beaten out on the old plowshare that hung from the chinaberry tree, clouds were already beginning to darken the northwest horizon. We hurriedly covered our last row of seeds, then headed for the cabin, where Nellie and Mom Allie presided over the cooking.

By the time we were all washed and seated, a riffle of cool breeze was interrupting the sultry heat of the morning. We ate with one eye turned skyward, expecting to be forced inside at any moment, but as it happened the storm didn't arrive until later. Yet all the time those blue-black clouds approached from the northwest, Lantana was uneasy as a fox in a box. She kept prowling onto the back porch and gazing first to the northwest, then to the southwest, then returning to her tasks in the cabin.

Skinny finally suggested that all those who lived at the house had better make tracks, while they could make it. Lantana shook her head, and to my surprise Mom Allie and Lucas agreed with her.

"Don't like the color of that sky," Lucas explained. "I think we'd better stick close to the Burrow, all of us. I feel a tornado, off there someplace."

"But it's not the season!" I stared at him in surprise. "We always have our tornadoes in the late fall and winter around here. Not in the dead of summer."

"Mostly," he agreed. "But not always, not even before

the bombs fell and did whatever they've done to the jet stream and the lay of the land, and maybe even the ocean currents. There's so much that we don't know now about how things are over the horizon. Anyway, my bones have lived with East Texas weather for a lot of years, and you can hardly fool 'em."

By now all of us were beginning to feel the electric prickle of the oncoming turbulence. A spatter of big, fat raindrops was followed by a gust of wind that laid the whole forest that we could see into a deep bow. It hit the cabin like a blow from a plank, and we all looked at one another, gathered up the children, handwork, and current books and retired to the cramped confines of the Burrow.

You haven't lived until you have crammed ten adults and nine children into a mobile home, however large and comfortable it might seem to be. Aside from lack of room, the young ones were wild with the excitement that accompanies an electrical storm. We finally had to let them out into the warm rain that now came down in opaque sheets. A little of that calmed them down, and we had them dried and drowsy when Lantana cocked her head, her old-fashioned corn-row braids standing out stiffly.

"Here she comes," she whispered.

It sounded like a train or a flight of jets. The rumble wasn't placeable as to direction, but we knew it must be coming up the track from southwest to northeast, for that was the almost invariable road the twisters took.

"God, let it bounce high off the last line of hills," murmured Mom Allie, and I added my silent amen to that. The painfully scrounged array of equipment and foodstuffs, books and clothing and tools we had labored to assemble could go, leaving no trace of anything that might be suspected of being a habitation. I'd seen it many times.

We had the windows open, for existence inside the Burrow with so many confined there was intolerable otherwise. Suddenly, there was a feeling of disorientation. The Burrow filled with green leaves, ripped from their moorings, then with hay. Our ears popped.

There seemed to be too little air, for a moment, but Zack staggered up and opened the door. A terrible cloud was moving over us, we could tell, but now rain to make the first seem a simple shower came bucketing down.

"Don't go out, son," Mom Allie said firmly. "You can't see anything yet. And any tree that was unbalanced by the wind may just decide to fall on down under the rain. You just sit here and sweat it out with the rest of us. But I'd guess that it came over about treetop high, right here. Though it may have touched down in one of the hayfields. Let's just pray that it missed the cabin and the house."

Outside, early though it was, it was dark as Egypt, as my father used to say. Then, gradually, the cloud lightened to a purplish-gray, and visibility returned to some extent, though curtained by the pouring rain. Lightning was flashing and booming away to the north of us, and we knew that it followed the track of the twister.

The children were totally subdued. Even Jim, who had been feeling himself to be quite grown up and competent, seemed content to be a little boy again, leaving the worrying to us. Every adult lap was occupied more than once during our wait, and the warm weight of the children comforted me, at least, as much as it reassured them to be near.

It wasn't as long as it seemed—it couldn't have been that long—until the rain eased to a lighter pattering, and the sky lightened even more. We straggled out into the wet and the mud and looked about.

A section of wood to the west had its top sheared as neatly as if a lawnmower had run over it, just below the tops of the trees. Hay was everywhere, and we knew that some, at least, of our haystacks had gone, literally, with the wind. A big white oak had toppled over the embankment into which we had dug the Burrow, though farther along. Its shattered top lay lower than its pitifully bare roots.

We picked our way around it and looked toward the cabin. It still stood, hunched low within its dirt bastions, though we could see that some of the sheets of tin had been ripped off the roof. That, however, might not have done so much damage, for we had put it on over the old shingle roof. As I hurried in and up the ladder to the loft, I found that there was not very much damp, even after the downpour we had had. And the books were safe.

As we muddled about, moving things from under drips and covering things too big to move, there came the blast of a shotgun from the rear of the house. Suzi, who had elected to help me in the cramped area under the roof, looked at me with terror in her eyes.

"They couldn't—they wouldn't—not on the heels of such a terrible storm—would they?"

I shook my head. Even the Ungers, I felt sure, had been driven to shelter by the wind and rain. No, whatever had brought about that blast from one of our own men folk was something else. I felt it in my bones.

Nonetheless, we both scuttered down the ladder and through the cabin in record time. Zack met us at the back door, gun in hand.

"Came a shot from over Fanchers' way. Then three more, spaced out like signals. You and Lucas come with me. The horses are spooked off into the woods, so we'd better run." He turned to Suzi. "Get some first-aid stuff together, spare bedding, whatever anybody might need, and send the kids out to find Maud. Then follow with Josh and Elmond."

She nodded and turned back into the house, while I slipped off my sandals and donned my heavy shoes, then shouldered the lighter rifle and sighed, "Ready!"

We started off at a trot. It was only a bit over a half mile to Fanchers' by our new route, but the grass and weeds were heavy with wet, and the spaces between were slippery with mud. Only after we reached the beaten-down grasses of the fields could we really make time. Even as we ran I could see, before us and to our right, that the ragged line of trees that marked the edge of the river wood had become much more ragged. There were big gaps, and I knew that we would find, when we had time to look, that windrows of trees would mark out the path where the tornado had dipped.

One of Annie's younger children waited for us beside the pathway. "Over to Londowns'," she cried, taking off in front of Zack.

Without slowing, we followed her as she led us off the trail, up a cow path, and to the edge of the Londowns' garden before we realized we were near.

The place was chaos compounded. Confetti-like debris

covered the area where the house had been, as well as the yard, garden, and even the fields around. Part of the orchard was gone. As we came to a halt I gripped Zack's hand tightly. I didn't want to know what we were about to learn.

A stifled shriek moved us to action. We pushed our way through the foliage of a downed elm and found Annie lying full-length on top of Cheri Londown, who was struggling and heaving to shake her off. The woman's eyes were blank, and one arm flopped as she squirmed.

"Knock her out, Zack," Annie panted. "She's hurt pretty bad, but she doesn't feel it. All she can do is worry about her husband. Bill's looking for him, right now, and the children."

Zack dropped to his knees, found an opportunity, and struck a solid blow beneath the woman's chin. She went out instantly, and I helped Annie to straighten her limbs, very carefully, feeling for the grating of bone.

Annie laughed hysterically. "One thing—I don't think there's a thing wrong with her spine. The way she fought and wiggled, it's got to be all right."

It was, but her left arm, her left leg, and several ribs were broken. What might have been simple fractures had been compounded by her desperate efforts to rise and look for her family, and we looked with dismay at the protruding bone poking through the arm. Then we pulled the limb straight, returning the bone as nearly as we could to its normal position, and Zack strapped it tightly to her side with his belt, my shirttail, and Annie's big red bandanna. Then we set out to find the others, though we did it with dreadful misgivings.

Someone must have had some warning. We found the three children crying silently and shivering in a drain ditch that ran through the orchard. They were frightened out of their wits, but we could find nothing but scratches and bruises on them, and we thought those came from their scramble into the ditch. Not one of them could talk coherently, so we carried them, even Carl, who was as big as his mother or bigger, back to her side and left them there with stern orders to watch her and not to let her move.

Then we heard a hail from the scrub oak patch just north of the house-place. We ran through the drizzle, wet bushes slapping into our faces and wet brambles catching our legs as we went toward Bill's call.

The little wood was of recent growth. There wasn't a tree more than fifteen or twenty feet tall. It was a good thing, for something that looked more like a scarecrow than a man was entangled in the top branches where three of the trees had interlocked their limbs. As I was lightest, Zack hoisted me into the lower branches, and I scrambled upward, cursing the maze of twisty growth that impeded my way.

I had hoped that the tangle that held Curt Londown would he flexible enough so that my added weight would bend it down. It was rigid as welded iron. With a sigh, I crawled out into the mess. One red-streaked arm came within my grasp, and I put my fingers on the pulse. There was one, very faint.

"He's alive," I yelled. "I'm going to have to have a saw or an axe, though, for I can't get to him, with all this junk wrapped around like it is."

I felt the tree shake, and I wiggled backward out of the way as Zack cut his way toward me with a hatchet that Bill must have produced. I watched anxiously as he began carefully cutting away the meshing branches that held Londown captive. It was entirely possible that any joggling, much less a fall from the treetop, would prove fatal to a man who had been thrown into a treetop by a tornado.

Below us, Bill, too, was worrying. I could see his wet face, turned upward. To ease us both, I asked, "Did you see the cloud coming? We just crawled into the Burrow and waited it out."

"Sure did," he answered. "We'd been eatin' when we heard the noise. Annie took the children and put 'em in the basement—mighty nice to have one, too. I never saw a house with one in this country, until this'n. Anyway, I stood at the door and watched 'er come. Three tails, she had. Just dippin' and slashin' down with lightnin' and thunder fit to drive you out of your mind. I took one look and went down with the others. I'm not brave when it comes to twisters."

"I wonder why the Londowns didn't all get in the ditch together?" l mused.

"Dumb bastard didn't think even a tornado would dare

mess with him," grunted Zack over his shoulder. "Can you come around the other side of the trunk and get hold of his other arm? It's hanging down about my knee level."

Once I had a grip on the other arm, we eased the limp bulk of the man, branch by branch, down the tree, cutting away anything that held up the process. Bill was waiting to hold him steady while we let him down the last of the way, and I prayed we hadn't punctured a lung with a broken rib or anything even worse.

When we had him flat on the leaf mold of the wood, we caught our breaths in horror. The man had practically been skinned. Aside from having on nothing but sneakers, he was almost denuded of hair and skin and even strips of flesh. Afraid to touch him, we waited for the wagon.

CHAPTER SEVENTEEN

There was only one thing to do. The Londowns, willy or nillv, must be divided up among those best able to care for them. Once we got Curt into the wagon, we dared not delay. We took him straight to the Jessups and Sim Jackman, picking up Lantana as we went back by the site of the destroyed house, where she was salvaging what she could. She was our best nurse, and we knew that Carrie and the girls would need her.

Bill and Annie were making Cheri ready to travel the short way to their own new dwelling. They had decided that she would be more biddable with one of her children to keep her company, so they took Cookie with them. Our own crew gathered up Carl and Carol and bore them back to the Burrow before they had a chance to come apart at the seams. In the twinkling of an eye, as it says in the Bible, the touch-me-not Londowns had become our care and responsibility. It was almost frightening.

"Remind me not to get to thinking we're sufficient unto ourselves," I said to Zack as we squelched along behind the slow-moving wagon. "It doesn't seem to be safe anymore."

"The hand of God," said Lantana over the still lump that was Curt Londown. "This fellow, he gets to thinking he's the best thing God ever turned a hand to, better than all the rest. Gets to thinking he can take care of anything comes along, no matter what. Just give him a gun in his pocket, and not Ungers nor niggers will dare to bother him. But Old Man Twister, he just waltzed right in and tore right out again."

"It scares me to death," I admitted, and I felt Zack's hand tighten on mine. "We always knew we could count on having droves of people come tearing in, when anything like this happened, and they'd try their best to save whoever could be saved, get things in shape, everything. I guess this, more than anything, makes me feel lonesome. That was one of the few good things about the world as it was."

"What's tearing me up," said Zack in a carefully emotionless voice, "is the notion that there may be folks all up and down the country, hurt and homeless, children wet and in shock, and nobody to come. Makes me wish we had ten times the people, so we could send some out scouting along the right directions to see if anybody needs help."

I shuddered, and not only with the wet chill of my ripped shirt and pants. Then I scrunched up under his arm, put my right hand in his left pocket, and said, "We're doing what we can, honey. There are so few people now, surely it won't have hit any more. Seldom did they make a long track of destruction, even when the country was full of folks."

He said nothing, and we walked along, sharing what little warmth we had between us. The alcohol lantern Lantana had lighted swung from the stanchion we had built onto the wagon, and our shadows wavered in monstrous shapes beside us as we forged ahead to warn the Jessups of a new influx of wounded.

The warm light of their lamp guided us the last few hundred yards, and Zack stopped to hail them before getting too close. "Ho, the Jessups!" Three times he called.

After the first hail, the lamp went out, leaving us with only the unsteady will-o'-the-wisp of the lantern far behind us. Then Horace's voice boomed, "That you, Zack?"

They were wonderful people. Before ten words had passed, they understood enough to have Grace rouse Sim from his after-supper nap, Laura lighting extra lamps and firing up the cook-stove, and their long-suffering table stripped, once again, for action.

"You should put up a sign—Jessup Hospital and Nursing Home," I laughed. "We come in here every few months, bringing desperately injured people. It's a wonder you don't shoot us on sight."

"We know that if we blow our horn, you'll be here as fast as feet can bring you," Carrie answered. "We may have lost the greater community that everybody depended on, but we seem to have landed on our feet with this smaller, closer, maybe more caring one. We may not have all the life-saving things that used to be available, but you know, child, dying isn't all that bad a thing. We used to know that. Sometimes it's a pure blessing just to die."

"But not if we can help it," I gritted, as the wagon groaned to a stop and Maud whuffed disapproval through her nostrils. Like it or not, Sim was the nearest thing we had to a doctor.

Luckily, our needs, up to now, had been in his line—accident and gunshot wounds. What we'd do when somebody came up with a hot appendix I hated to think, but until that time we'd make do with Sim's rough skills.

The old man came out of his bedroom, hair on end, looking like the sort of stick figure first-graders used to draw. He sighed when he saw me.

"Don't take it amiss, Miz Hardeman," he drawled, "but whenever I see you I look past you for whoever's near dead this time."

"Curt Londown," I said, opening the door for Zack and Horace to carry the slack figure inside. We had laid him in a sheet that Suzi brought in the wagon, and they carefully maneuvered him, sheet and all, onto the table. The cloth was streaked with blood now. The man on it seemed flayed.

"Fore God!" Sim whispered. "I don't know, folks. I've seen a man bit by alligators, tore by a bobcat, but this 'un—this 'un is bad."

Lantana edged by him with a basin of warm water. "Got to get this mess off, before we can see to tend him," she grunted. "Then we'll know can we do or can we don't."

It seemed impossible that Londown's chest could still be rising and falling. Still, he was breathing fairly regularly, and his heart was beating, though slowly. As Lantana's ministrations removed the crusted blood, the extent of his lacerations seemed to worsen. Sim bent over him, his monkey-like face screwed up with concern, and suddenly the man's eyes opened.

"The wind..." he mouthed, though no voice came through.

"Twister's gone now, son," said Sim, and Lantana laid her dark hand on Curt's forehead as his pale eyes turned up toward her. "The Fanchers—they came?" His voice was less than a croak.

Zack answered him. "They came. They signaled for us to come, too. They're taking care of your wife, who isn't too badly hurt, and the children, who are all fine."

The pale eyes closed for a moment, then opened. "Don't eat crow worth a damn," he said clearly. Blood spilled from the corner of his mouth, and he was gone.

We looked across the pool of lamplight at one another. My face must have held the shock that marked all the others, for it seemed almost as if the man had chosen to die rather than to give up his dearly held beliefs.

Carrie folded the edges of the sheet together over the mutilated body. Tears were running down her cheeks, but her hands were steady as she covered the face, first closing the blank eyes.

"We tried," she said to Horace as she turned into his arms. "It just wasn't enough."

"His lungs must of been tore up," Sim muttered, wiping his eyes on his sleeve. "Couldn't have fixed him up, anyway, Miss Carrie. He was too far gone. It's just that there's so damn few of us any more."

We buried him that night. It was a weird procession, by lantern light, but we took him to the Sweetbriers' and laid him beside Jess. Somehow, we hated to think of him lying alone, and we felt that this would perhaps comfort Cheri.

It didn't, though. We had, of course, known Cheri even less than we had Curt. None of us had ever heard her open her mouth and utter words, even. We just took it for granted that she was something like the rest of us, determined to survive and to make her children survive. We weren't prepared for the reality of Cheri Londown.

I've known a few people—two women and one man, actually—who were fairly decent and acceptable people, seemingly. All three had been married to (or the child of) one person who had the reputation of being hard and strict to the point of cruelty. In the cases I knew, when the dominant person was suddenly removed (by death, in my cases), this ostensibly equable person suddenly became hell on wheels. Unreasonable, demanding, arbitrary. All the worst traits you can think of.

Cheri made them all look like pikers.

Her injuries were severe enough to keep her immobile for quite a while, though luckily she developed no infections. When she had been with the Fanchers a week, Annie made the trek to Hickory Hollow to pour out her woes. "She thinks we're there to fetch for her. Got nothing else to do, she thinks. Yells at the babies, gets onto her own child until I could cry for the little thing. She's a miserable person, Luce. What we going to do?"

"I'll swap you the other two children for her," I offered. "They are bright kids. Once they realized their dad was dead and their house really gone for good, they buckled to and changed their ideas. I don't think you'll have a bit of trouble with them. They get along fine with all our bunch, now."

"But what'll you do with Cheri? She's a pill, I tell you."

"I'll turn her over to Lantana and Mom Allie. Did you ever see somebody break a colt to the plow by hitching him between two big mules? He'll do his best to buck and snort, but the wise old heavyweights just amble along without even knowing he's there. I can't see Cheri having the spunk to even tackle the two of them, much less bother either one."

First, of course, I consulted my "mules." They laughed at the notion, but both agreed to try their hand at civilizing our invalid. As the cabin was now less closely tenanted since the children had moved out, we put her in Lisa's old pantry bedroom. Though it seemed sheer callousness, I felt that we might as well get the idea across to her, soon and early, that she was an added burden, not an honored guest. That tight, dark cubicle should tell her something, I thought.

It did. Then she told us, at length and at the top of her voice. Complete with obscenities that I had thought well lost with the outside world. When I finished washing out her mouth, I grabbed the foot of the army cot on which she lay, Lantana took the head, and we zipped her out of the house, down the back yard, and behind the smokehouse.

"Now you can say just what you think," Lantana said sternly, "without contaminatin' our ears. We'll check on you, now and again, to make sure you're all right. And when you think you can behave, we'll bring you back inside." Then, turning to me, she asked, "Have we got an old tarp we can throw over her if it rains?'

We left her screaming after us. I, for one, felt like a villain, but I knew this was necessary. She must either shape up or be sent out.

She was brought back inside three days later. Her head, be it known, was the harder sort. She kept thinking, every time one of us went down to feed her or to help her relieve herself, that she could talk us into submission. It wasn't until we left her out in the rain all night that she capitulated. It wasn't a real storm, thank heaven, but even a light drizzle must seem like a cloudburst when you lie out under a tarp and hear it pattering on top of you for five or six hours.

After that, she quieted down and stopped demanding. Still, I'd catch a strange expression on her face now and again, and I'd wonder. She looked just like old Rock, my dad's setter, who would never dream of killing a chicken—as long as we were watching.

She healed quickly, though her arm would never be exactly straight, and she had lost some motion in it. The ribs gave her trouble for a long time, probably as a result of her struggle when they were first broken. But her leg mended without trouble, and she was able to walk fairly soon, for Skinny and Josh built her a walker out of old pipe.

We were all, understand, busy as ticks in a tar bucket, all the time. Our efforts on her behalf were matters of a few minutes here and there, taken from our scanty leisure. And while she had ceased her demands, I never had the feeling that she truly understood her situation. Mom Allie's three dressings-down, delivered to Cheri in no uncertain terms, were enough, I felt, to keep her in line for a long time to come. But she didn't really understand. You could see it in her face.

They must have been a strange household, the Londowns. Curt sure that he was God's anointed, and Cheri certain that she was the exact center of the universe. How the three young ones could have come out of it as nearly sensible as they had done was a wonder.

As Cheri became well, our problems increased. It wasn't that she refused to work. She just didn't. A pan of potatoes left for her to peel would sit there until someone else grabbed it up and tended to it. She hated to wear her clothes more than once. We had come to terms with the matter—we could either be immaculate or get the important work done, not both. For her there was no question. She must have clean clothes, and the fact that the clothes were Suzi's made no difference.

At last, I reversed Annie's journey and took my problem to her. She listened to my tale with a grave face. "Whatever we do with her, Luce, we mustn't put her back with her kids," she said when I had finished. "The one thing in the world they were scared to death of was their mother. Not their dad. I've sat and rocked little Cookie more nights than one when she got to thinking about her dad being gone. Carl and Carol loved him. Really loved him. But you want to see faces go pale as ghosts, just ask them if they want to go visit their mom."

Well, that was that. I'd thought of setting up the remainder of the family in Nellie's house, after proper work was done on it, of course, with maybe Elmond or Josh as live-in father figure.

But now I saw that it wouldn't do at all. It had begun to look as if we were going to have an albatross hung around our necks, for good and all.

However, once she had regained her strength and agility, she solved the problem for us. She ran away.

CHAPTER EIGHTEEN

At first, it was a great relief. Though we did worry, of course, about her and checked downriver to see if she had taken refuge with the Jessups or the Fanchers. She was no place we looked. We even saddled a couple of horses, Suzi and I, and went up the little-used road toward Mrs. Yunt's house, checking the bare patches of earth for tracks now and again.

Mrs. Yunt's house was just as we had left it, plus a winter of emptiness. Though it was a stoutly built place, clapboard laid over the original log structure, it had a look as if the starch had somehow gone out of it. Obviously, nobody had been near it since the last time we had checked it.

We rode on up the road, around the persimmon sprouts that were springing up in its middle, over the Bermuda grass that was encroaching onto its surface from the ditches. Grandpa Harkrider's house was gone. Burned down to fine ash, the shrubbery about it withered and dead on the side next to the house.

"Lightning?" asked Suzi, as we drew rein in the front yard and looked at the devastation.

"Maybe," I answered. "Or possibly Ungers. Grandpa's fields go right on back to the river. It makes a big loop here, before swinging west just south of our place. If those hellions use the river for their road, it would make sense. I often wonder why they didn't burn poor Nellie alive when they raided her place."

Suzi looked down across the fields that were now visible with the removal of the house. Her delicate face looked very oriental as she said carefully, "It may be...that was their first.

They had not yet...refined...their techniques."

A forgotten fact popped into my mind. Suzi had been a psychology major at the University of Colorado when she met her husband. She, if any of us, would probably know the proper terminology for the Ungers' aberrations. Then I dismissed the thought. Terms are irrelevant; it's effects that count. And preventive measures.

The same thought came to us simultaneously. We recognized its shape as we looked, eye into eye, considering the appalling notion.

"She has gone to the Ungers." I don't know which of us breathed the words.

We turned our mounts and fled back down the road as fast as was safely possible. We knew that we must lay this terrible possibility before the others as soon as we could, for Cheri knew, from the inside out, our defenses. Ours and Fanchers', though not, praise be, the Jessups'.

We rousted our clan from field and garden, house and barn and wood, young and old together. And once they realized what we were saying, they were as intent as we.

"I'll lay odds you're right," sighed Lucas. "She used to listen real close when we talked about 'em. Could be she thinks she's smart enough to walk in down there and take over where the death of the old Unger left a gap. Have a whole swarm of slaves at her command. Come back, maybe, and make us pay for expectin' her to behave like a human bein'. That little gal lacked somethin'...somethin' I can't rightly put my finger on, but necessary."

Our first order of business seemed obvious. We must do our best to make the complex defensible. And knowing our adversaries' penchant for attack with fire, we must make our defenses unburnable. Two crews began work on that immediately. All the children except Joseph, who was elected overseer, divided themselves into bucket brigades under Elmond's and Skinny's supervision.

The two men dug down to the red clay in two spots, one near the cabin, one not too far from their own house. Then the children hauled buckets full (or as full as they could carry) of water and dumped them into the clay holes until the men could mix up a good red glop of mud. The rest of us hauled buckets of mud and daubed the stuff onto everything. Every exposed inch of wood in the two dwellings was covered thickly. Not just once, but over and over until it was thick as adobe. Luckily, both houses had overhanging eaves, which would keep the rain from doing much damage over the short haul. And we had other plans for the long haul.

By the time we were finished, we and the houses both looked like complete messes. However, the stuff dried to a pleasant sandy red color, and we shaped it by scraping off lumps and blobs, rounding corners smoothly, and squaring it off about the windows. In two days we had things fairly well squared away. We had also built an earthwork, using the slip and old Maud, across the approach from the creek and the river. It wasn't too high, but it was thick enough to stop a slug, we hoped.

Then we set our other plan into motion. The stills, being sun-heated, worked all the summer at top speed. We had big batches of mash cooking off every day, to be replaced in the fermenting vats by mushy potatoes, overripe watermelons, green cornstalks, extra beans, and vines...anything and everything that grew and would ferment. The stills worked all day, every day, fueling the tillers, the old tractor, even the lanterns that lighted our nightly prowlings. They also made Molotov cocktails.

We worked doubly, now, for our regular labors couldn't be neglected. Our survival depended on keeping up with the harvesting, preserving, sewing, wood gathering that would make our winter livable. But those fermenting barrels and stills were our first order of duty.

One morning, while swilling out the biggest barrel, I had an idea. "Let's fuel up the big tractor rig that we used to bring in the Burrow and pull it right into the middle of the driveway, just in the narrow part of the bend between the embankment and the swampy spot. That will stop anybody from coming at us in a bunch from that direction. I'd feel better with that route bottled up."

Nellie, who was working with me, nodded "Soon as we're through," she grunted, rolling one barrel aside and beginning on another.

When Zack saw what we had done, later, he grinned.

"Good thinking," was all that he said, but later he told me, "I'm glad you got it running and out so that we can move around in it. I'm thinking that we need a boat."

"We have a boat," I objected.

"I mean a big boat. Maybe a catamaran. One that will take a bunch of us downriver, slide low on the current. Ride over a lot of the logs and debris. Down to the lake. One that will, if need be, take off like a scalded cat."

I looked at him, and my heart began to thud uncomfortably "You mean to go downriver." It wasn't a question.

"Got to, Luce. We can't wait for them to come at us, choosing their own time and opportunity. No, tomorrow I'm going after a boat, if I have to go all the way to Nicholson."

"You won't have to, I said. "I'll bet you anything you like that the Greens had several boats, all of them the best money can buy. Everything else they had was the best and most expensive of its kind—why should their boats be any different? Where there is a boathouse the size of theirs, there are boats, believe me."

We headed out the next morning, by the road. Once more we found ourselves on the oil-top, passing those places whose rear approaches had become so familiar to us. We stopped at the Jessups' to pick up Horace. He had keys to everything, it seemed.

We'd never been down the drive beneath that ornate gateway. It was covered with white shell that had obviously been kept neatly edged. The house itself was a red-brick monstrosity.

The tall blank façade faced the road, with narrow windows and stingy portico giving it a disapproving expression. The blinds were closed, and I could imagine the musty smell of mildew that must hang inside that stuffy building.

We followed the drive around the sweeping arc to the back. Strictly ornamental stables and pergolas cluttered up what should have been a clean sweep of magnificent view to the river.

I decided that I wouldn't have liked the Greens very much.

As we drove up to the boathouse, I asked Horace, "Why in thunder haven't the Ungers raided this place? I'd think it would tempt them past endurance."

He laughed. "There were always watchmen. Right until the blowup. The Greens had them here, day in, day out, around the clock. Everybody on the river knew better than to look cross-eyed at this place." He grunted and looked out toward the mud-brown water.

"I can't prove it, but I happen to know that somebody tried to come in the back way to rob this place, a couple of years ago. Got shot doing it. The bodies went into the river and came up in the lake. It got credit for being a hunting accident, but I knew the men. They weren't hunters. They were thieves. I sat on juries when both of them were tried, the year before. We sentenced them, but they were out before you could say scat." He spat as he opened the door.

"Anyway, the Ungers aren't bright. It hasn't dawned on them that things have changed so much that there aren't any watchmen anymore. They're gone, but those dimwits haven't figured it out and probably won't."

We found three boats in the boathouse. The catamaran was slung for repair, but Zack fell in love with a low, fast-looking fiberglass job whose motor kicked over the first time he touched the switch. That was, of course, the last breath of the battery, but Horace heaved on the manual starter while Zack nursed the engine along, until both were satisfied that it was in good shape.

We went home in triumph, pulling the boat behind our rig on a custom-built trailer.

We put the whole thing, temporarily, up in Grandpa Harkrider's garden. Then we took the truck back and plugged up our drive again. By then it was mid-afternoon.

Zack called a meeting of the clan when everyone came in for supper from various chores around the farm. "We've got to make up our minds as to what we're going to do," he said to Mom Allie. "We can't just let those bitches keep chewing up anybody they've a mind to. I want to hit them, all together, one great big go-for-broke lick."

Mom Allie didn't say a word, though I realized that Zack kept watching her out of the corner of his eye when he thought she wasn't looking. That told me that he was worried about her reaction to his proposal. She had always had a thing about turning the other cheek. But I thought that he was mistaken, this time. Mom Allie had a good eye for survival.

We cleared away the debris of the meal. We had eaten on the tables we had built under the trees in the back yard, and once we'd settled down all eyes turned toward Zack. He looked troubled and seemed to have a problem thinking how to begin.

Lucas spoke before Zack could. "I think most of us know what's on your mind, Zack. It's been on ours, too, for a while. Since before the Fanchers got burned out, that's for sure. We've been havin' some of the same problem that I think you've been sweating. Been talking it over a lot. It's not the same world it was, you know, in a lot of ways we haven't even discovered yet. Tell him, Alice."

Mom Allie fiddled with a sweetgum leaf that had settled beside her plate while Lucas was speaking. She didn't look happy, but then again she didn't look incurably depressed, either. It took her a minute to get her thoughts together, but we all waited quietly.

"Look, son," she began at last, "I know I taught you patience and forbearance and brotherly love and turning the other cheek. In the world we had then, that was good, sound sense, no matter how little anybody else lived by it. I think you managed to live a full and happy life because of those teachings, even with Vietnam and that time in Houston subtracted from the total. Those things were true then, and they're true now...to a certain extent. They'll be true again, completely. Someday."

Another leaf planed down and settled into Lisa's lap. It was the cool green that only sweetgum achieves, and Lisa held it to her cheek while she listened.

"Now we've got to make a new life from scratch. There are problems we never thought we'd have to cope with, and one of 'em is the Ungers. They are going to kill us all out, family by family, person by person, house by house, if we leave them to their own devices and just wait for them to choose their own time and place to hit us. When you told me that this afternoon, I knew it was true, even if I hated to admit it. Now we've had a chance to talk it over, we old ones.

We're with you, all the way." She looked at him for a moment, and her eyes looked sad behind her glasses.

"Get together with Bill, why don't you? The two of you saw a lot of action overseas. Sneaky, double-dealing kinds of war. That's what we need. We can't afford to waste decent lives on cleaning out that trash."

Skinny cleared his throat. So seldom did he venture to speak when we all were together that everyone turned to him in surprise.

"That damn Cheri's with 'em, too. Don't ever forget that. She knows our defenses. She knows the way we go about doing things. She was smart, that one, no matter how side-slung her mind was. If she's gone off to them Ungers, she's got some kind of plan for getting back at us. The only reason they ain't wiped us out, before now, is that they didn't have no brains. Now they got one. Don't forget that."

And that was the last nail in the box. We knew that, much as we didn't want to admit it. The danger that had been intermittent would probably become constant. Nobody could afford to go off on a job in the woods or the far fields without several people with him. Our manpower didn't stretch that far.

I looked at Zack. "Tomorrow you can go see Bill."

He shook his head. "I'm going to blow the trumpet. I want to see Bill and Horace tonight. I'll go to meet them, to save time. You cover me, Luce, from the last fencerow. There's almost a full moon. There'll be enough light."

We left the others to do the last of the evening chores. And I watched Zack trudge away across the fields toward Bill's house with my heart thumping uneasily. The trumpet blast had brought a faint answer from Horace's end of the line, so we knew Bill had heard. Before Zack reached the second fence, I saw a dim shape moving toward him from the direction of Fanchers'. They went together to meet Horace, and I stretched myself in the honeysuckle of the fencerow to wait for their return.

They were well out of sight, and I was mulling over the myriad things I needed to do tomorrow besides going to war, when I heard a sound. It wasn't a whippoorwill. Almost, but not quite. An inexpert whistler was trying for that call.

Someone was watching the men move away across the fields. I sat, very slowly and cautiously, and eased the barrel of the 30.06 through the vines to cover the area behind the fence. But nobody moved into the field from the dark bulk of the river woods. Whoever it was had been sending a signal to someone else. And that was a much brighter thing than the Ungers had ever been known to do.

CHAPTER NINETEEN

Though I watched until my eyes created their own illusions, there was no movement in the fields until Zack's tall shape came glimmering toward me in the moonlight. I hissed at him before he could speak to me and betray the fact that I had been there, and he opened the wire gap in the fence, closed it firmly, and set off up the path toward the cabin. In a few minutes, I slid into the deepest shadow I could find and followed. Nobody had moved into our woods that I could detect.

It was late. The moon was high, and all the children were safely asleep in the Burrow when we gathered about the table in the cabin for our parley of war. Bill had had the idea that we felt was most useful.

"We're going to set up an ambush. It'll take some doing, but we want to draw those who are watching the houses down toward their own headquarters. Then we want to bring them all pelting upriver, so mad and excited that they aren't thinking. Which isn't that hard to do, Cheri or no Cheri," he sighed. "The question is, what will be so irresistible that they just can't help following us to see what we do with it?"

"Whiskey!" said Lantana, firmly. "They ain't got sense enough to make their own—never did. The old Unger'd buy from moonshiners all up and down the river. Now they're all gone, nobody there to get it from, I'll bet those women are havin' shakes and pink elephants and everything that goes with it. Probably had enough for months stashed away. But I'll bet they haven't got much left by now. Whiskey would bring 'em runnin', I just bet."

Well, I'd thought guns, and I could see that Zack had

thought of food. But given the Unger mentality—if you can call it that—whiskey was probably the very thing.

"But all our stuff is in fruit jars. How will they know what it is?" That was Nellie, practical as ever.

Mom Allie burst into laughter. "You remember how shocked Vera was when I insisted on bringing home all those empties from behind the Starlight Bar in Nicholson? I thought then, and I still do, that a glass bottle will be worth its weight in gold, until somebody can come up with a glass factory again. I've got ten cases of whiskey bottles sitting behind the cabin in the old tool shed, right now. Labels and all. Won't even have to waste our alcohol, either. It's clear as water. Might as well be water."

We got up very early the next morning and filled bottles. By the time the sun was well up, we had four cases, which was about all that the new boat could haul, along with several adults.

"Where should be the best place to put the boat into the water and load the cargo?" Zack asked Skinny.

"Back when I was bootleggin'," that worthy replied, "we used to run our moonshine up to Boggy Slough. There's a good slope to the riverbank there, good for puttin' boats in, and for puttin' things into boats as well. Everybody all up and down the river knowed that Boggy Slough was the place to watch, if you wanted to know what was goin' on."

"You suppose the Ungers still watch it?"

"I'd guess the old 'un kept a lookout there all the time. Probably they never have realized that now she's gone and they don't have to do what she told 'em anymore."

Well, given the Ungers, that made some sense. Boggy Slough wasn't too far from the present location of the boat, either. Back behind Grandpa Harkrider's place in that big loop.

Zack looked at me. "If this works, you're going to have to organize the ambush. There's a narrow spot in the river just below the Greens' boathouse. The land's still fairly well cleared all the way down to the water on our side of the river, then there's thick woods just this side of it. Anybody trying to catch up with a boat on the water will be pelting along the river track and will have to come out into that clearing. It'll be...like shooting fish in a barrel."

I shook my head. "Nothing's that easy," I said. "But I'll tend to things at this end. You get the whiskey loaded and the boat moving. That ought to pick up every sentry Cheri's got posted along the line of houses. Who's going with you?"

"Skinny. Elmond used to fish every inch of the river along here, and he's going. The three of us ought to be enough. Once we get past your position, we'll tie the boat and come to help you. God, Luce! I hate this!"

I put my cheek against his. "I know. I didn't sign up to be an ambusher, either, but it looks as if that's what it's going to take."

Then the three men were gone, and I got busy getting our ambush going. Every child from our place and Fanchers' who was too small to shoot was barricaded into the Burrow. Lantana stood guard there, and I pitied anyone who might try to get past her. Sukie was a crack shot, but too small for our business, so she was the "rear guard" for the Burrow. That gave them a field of fire from both front and side. There wasn't another opening into the place.

We hitched up Maud to the wagon and took with us food, enough ammunition to start a good-sized war, every gun on the place except for those in the Burrow, and bedding. Just in case.

Also a lot of bandage material. But I refused to think about that.

Annie and Tony met us at the fence line, and we went together, though spread cautiously and taking advantage of the cover, along the upper reaches of the fields. That meant cutting more wire and making more gaps to keep the cattle in, but we had never used this way before, and we knew that we couldn't be seen from the river.

Bill and Horace met us at the Sweetbriers', and we cut out to the road, as that was shorter here. We all gathered at the Greens' house, invisible from the river because of the jumble of useless buildings. There were fifteen, counting Jim and Bill's Tony and Lisa. Not a bad little army, all things considered. While we waited for the boat to do its work of clearing away watchers, we assigned positions.

Sim had stayed at the Jessups', being simply unable to

move about fast enough to take part in an ambush. He had pots of water ready to boil and every clean rag available stacked up ready to make into bandages or compresses. Nellie elected to stay with him, as she was the world's poorest shot. Lisa, too, looked greenish and ill, and I went to her and put my arm around her.

"We have plenty of guns. Why don't you go and take care of Sim and Nellie for me? They'll need a pair of young legs to do their running. How about that?"

She looked up at me, her face grim and set, far too old for its years. "That...that'd be better. If you can do without me."

When I nodded, she looked as if she might faint with relief, and I packed her off with Nellie while internally blaming myself for letting her leave the Burrow in the first place. It hadn't reached the point, yet, when we would make a child kill its own family, no matter how that family deserved killing.

So that meant there would be fewer. Josh and Lucas behind us, because of their eyes. They were dead shots, but they couldn't see their prey until it got fairly close. Any we missed, they'd get, I knew. Mom Allie and Suzi and Horace we decided to dig into emplacements wherever the bank offered thick cover. Bill and Annie and Carrie and I would take the woods just past the clearing. We went up into that musty and dead-smelling house and peeped from upper windows to pick out exact locations. Then all we could do was wait for the boat to pass.

It came by about noon, and it was really moving, It put my heart into my throat to think what might happen to that fiberglass bottom if they hit a log end-on or hung a half-submerged stump. But Elmond was at the helm, and I knew that his eyes, old as they were, would put all the rest of us to shame. I caught a glimpse of Zack's long shape lying beside Skinny. From our high perch we could see down into the boat, which those along the embankment couldn't. The whiskey cases stood up boldly, proclaiming their famous brands to any who could read and their logos to those who might not. As I watched, I saw a distant figure step free of the trees to look after the speeding craft. Then she took out after it, her rifle trailing from a careless hand. In a minute, six more shapes bounded past, one after the other, following the lure we had set for them.

"You think that's all?" I asked Lucas.

He nodded. Then he added, "But let's wait another ten minutes, just to be on the safe side."

No more Ungers came past. So we went down and dug ourselves into cover, literally for our advance spotters, and at least partially for the rest of us. The cover was really good...thigh-sized young hickories grown up with stands of huckleberry and haw to make a screening blind that would have been the envy of any duck hunter.

That was the longest afternoon I ever spent in my life. As the sun went low and sank, I became less and less sure of our plan. In the dark, our firepower was going to be far less accurate. We were going to miss a lot of them…that was clear. While I tried to ease tense muscles without betraying my position, I was mulling over a back-up plan. Just in case it might be needed.

We heard the motor when it must have been at least a mile down the twisting course of the stream. The flutter came clearly at times, then was muffled by intervening forest. But that sound brought us all alert at once. We gave short, sharp whistles to indicate that we were awake and ready. Thirteen whistles, including mine. All in order. I fixed my eyes on the glint of the water in moonlight, the pale patch of dusty clearing.

With incredible suddenness, the boat zoomed into sight downriver, moving toward our position, the bow waves pearly white under the bright moon. It swished past us into the deep shadow of the overarched channel just behind us. The motors were cut, leaving sudden silence. Surely that might warn the pursuers!

But they were making so much noise, crashing through undergrowth and splashing into shallow spots at the river's edge that they evidently didn't hear that at all.

Our troops at the point were good, steady people. They held their fire and let the first group get into the clearing, dead in our sights. I knew that they'd take care of any stragglers that showed up in the next few minutes, and I took aim, waited for a half second of pure agony, and fired. One of the women threw up her hands and went down, upsetting a good handful of her companions. While they were sorting themselves out, all of those were picked off. Then we were firing into the bunch, and they were wriggling off into the brush behind them. There they met fire from Suzi and Horace and Mom Allie. Others were snaking into the river to get upstream. I knew that our rear guard would tend to them, along with Zack and his navy.

The clearing still seemed to swarm with struggling shapes. The moonlight was almost too bright. I hated to see the carnage we were making. And then something took my left leg from under me, and I hit my head as I went down against the tree I was using for a gun rest.

I came to to find Zack beside me, running his hands over me to find where I was hit. There was no sound of shooting at all.

"Left leg," I grunted. Then: "It's over?"

"This part is," he said, just as his fingers found the hole in my leg.

That took my mind off the battle for some time. Then I realized that I was hearing no moans or cries of pain.

"Surely we didn't kill them all dead?" I asked.

His face was in shadow, so I couldn't see his eyes. "Eventually," he gritted.

"Oh." Some things make being shot look suddenly worthwhile. I don't know if I could have given the *coup de grace* to a fallen enemy. Even Ungers.

Then there was a lot of pain and flashes of moonlight between periods of fainting. And at last I found myself on Carrie's kitchen table, looking up into Sim's monkey-like eyes. I could hear someone breathing very raggedly over toward the other table.

"Who?" I asked Sim, as he dolloped alcohol into my leg. I didn't catch his answer the first time around. Then I got it.

"Skinny?" I gulped. "How bad?"

"Pretty bad. Not that bad, now, Miz Hardeman. He ain't gonna die. Not unless we have some purely bad luck. But bad enough. You're not really hurt much a'tall. Just a little old leg wound and a bump on the head. And that's all. I'm really amazed. I thought I'd be patchin' up people until sunset tomorrow."

For a little old leg wound, it hurt an awful lot. I'd settle for that and not complain that I didn't get a hero's dose. But I was able to go home in the wagon next morning. Annie had got a pressure bandage on the leg as soon as Zack found it, so I didn't lose much blood. They told me that Skinny would have to stay put for a while. Poor Carrie. Her hospital was keeping up its reputation.

CHAPTER TWENTY

The ride home wasn't a bit of fun. To ease my mind, if nothing else, Zack told me the tale of his naval adventure. It had worked like a charm.

"I don't know if they had a watcher at the Slough or not," he said. "But they caught onto us before we'd gone a half mile downriver, which probably means that somebody was keeping an eye on the spot. Elmond was running the boat as if he were all alone in it. Skinny and I fixed us up a place to lie between the cases, with slits to look out of without being seen. I had the old field glasses Pa brought back from World War I, and I definitely saw two of them following us before we got down as far as our place. Then, of course, we were outdistancing them, because the channel got wider and there wasn't so much litter in the water. The river is still up a good bit from the last rain, so the snags were covered pretty well, and that is one shallow-draught boat.

"We just pelted along, and the closer we got to the lake, the more I got to wondering how we were going to stir up the big bunch of them. Finally, once we got out into the lake itself, we pulled over into some brush and had a parley. We decided that if we looked like somebody trying to locate other survivors, that might make them think we had something they wanted. That would make them chase us. And if we ran, they're too much like wild beasts not to tear out after us, just because we ran. That worked, too. We yelled and whooped and slapped each other on the backs when we came in sight of their houses. They were coming out of doorways and sliding out of the underbrush, staring at us with those white eyes. It was scary enough to make it seem really natural when Skinny yelled, 'Them's Ungers!'

"Then Elmond revved up the engine again, and we hit the river's channel with everything we had. We passed the bunch that had been chasing us about a mile and a half up-river. They just turned right around and took off again, with the rest coming after them. But I imagine the ones who'd run all the way down the river after us gave out before they got here. So that's one bunch we still have to reckon with."

"Do you have any idea how many there were of them—from the size of their place and the number you actually saw?" I asked him. Not that I cared, right then, but it was something to think of besides the hot poker up my leg.

"Must have been thirty or thirty-five, at least." He looked over his shoulder at me as I lay in the bed of the wagon. "We buried eighteen. Some that got away into the river and the woods were wounded. Those will likely die, unless they're mighty lucky. We...may have to lick this cat over again, some of these days."

I forgot the leg. I pulled myself up halfway, sitting so he could hear me clearly. "No. Now is the time to stop this thing in its tracks. Not that we can winkle out all the ones that have gone to earth in the woods. But we can stop it at the source. We've got to hit their compound, down there on the lake. Tomorrow, before any of them get their wits together and go back. The children, Zack! If we take away the children, there aren't any men around to give them any more. They'll die, and their whole stinking way of life will die with them. They won't be able to be anything but a minor nuisance, from here on out."

He turned on the seat and stared at me. Then he nodded, once, decisively. "You're right. Now's the time. But you can't go. No way!"

Zack and Lucas and Elmond and I went downriver the next morning. I'd made Lucas rig up Cheri's old walker for me, and once Zack understood that I'd walk, bad leg and all, if he didn't let me go in the boat, he gave in. The leg throbbed like all the toothaches in the world rolled into one, you understand, but something inside me had to go, no matter what.

The river channel hadn't ever been terribly wide. Rolling hills on both sides had held it in. But it was a fairly deep stream, mud-bottomed, as were all East Texas rivers and creeks for most of their length. Button willows lined the banks, and the larger willow trees waded out into the channel, making it narrower still. Water weeds and cattails grew in the shallows, and small islands of every size lay like alligators at every bend. We went slowly, and seeing the route made me cringe at the thought of the reckless speed with which Elmond had navigated the thing the day before.

We didn't use the motor, simply guiding the big boat with oars from our own rig, and fending off snags and drowned trees with the blades. The channel widened, and you could tell by the pull against the hull that the current was both swift and strong. Here we found ourselves among the snags and stumps of the forest that had been drowned when the catchment behind the dam had been filled.

Elmond tapped Zack on the shoulder. "Better pull in along here and sneak across that tongue of land to see if any of the Ungers have come back to the houses."

There was a narrow channel back into the button willows. Zack pulled us into it, and I waited there, holding the boat against the bank, while they crept away to reconnoiter. It seemed a long time. The sun was hot, reflecting off the water, and I pulled the boat further into the shadows of the bushes and cursed the leg that was now beginning to feel as if a cougar were gnawing on its bone.

In time the two returned, quietly as cats. I had the boat eased along the bank so they could step in by the time they reached me.

"Well?" I asked, pushing away from the bank.

"Nobody there. Not that we could see, and no smoke from the chimneys, either. We'll go right in. I don't think there's anyone there at all.

Zack maneuvered the boat back into the channel and cut its prow at an angle toward the bluff they had just negotiated.

We nosed into the lake and around the bluff, turning back to skirt the shoreline. I could see the shacks well before we reached them, and I understood why the making of the lake hadn't inundated them. They had been built right on the bluff that had been one bank of a creek, which had entered the old river at this point. Now the bluff was low, for the water came up its sides, but the houses were high and dry.

The compound was a ratty affair. Some ten houses stood there, every one looking as if a good sneeze might bring it down. We pulled into a ramp, and Zack lifted me out of the boat and handed me my walker.

As I grasped the walker, something came to my ears. Crying children...a lot of them. I swung awkwardly and began thumping toward the isolated hut that seemed to be the source of the sound. It was work, hopping and moving the walker and hopping again, but I made it to the small unglazed window in the shanty and looked through. Then I turned and vomited.

There were a dozen in there. A couple of infants lying on ragged quilts that covered the entire floor. Three toddlers under two. Seven more ranging in age from maybe three to four and a half. They were so filthy that the term meant nothing. Excrement was smeared over everything. They were all naked. Their bodies were crusted with sores and feces. When one of them looked up and saw my face at the window, it let out a howl and burrowed under the nearest of its companions. Then they all began to scream.

Leaning on the walker, I felt the weight of years and responsibilities. We were so few! And we were either very young or very old. We literally could not take on a dozen wild beasts to care for and civilize. It would kill Carrie. Grace and Laura were far from stable and perhaps never would be again. We hadn't dared let them too near the scene of the ambush yesterday.

Zack and I were responsible for nine children and ten old people. Bill and Annie had ten children to take care of already. It simply wasn't possible.

Neither was it possible to leave them there to become killers. I groaned aloud. Zack came up behind me and put his arms around me. I leaned my head back against him and thought harder than ever before in my life.

Given the fact of Lisa, I could see hope for them. If they were removed, right now, from this terrible place. If they were shared out among reasonably normal people, to grow up ignorant of their wild dams, they could probably become assets to our depleted world. They were desperately needed lives. We had to try to manage something for them.

"There must be people around the lake," I said to Zack. "Remember...Mom Allie said everyone who had a lake house had packed up and headed for it." I felt him nod. "It stands to reason that some of the places around the lake have people in them. If we can just get these children worked down to two or three, we may be able to manage.

Elmond's gruff voice made me open my eyes. "We'll sluice 'em down in the lake, Luce. Nobody could stand to look at 'em the way they are now. You just go and sit down on that choppin' block. We'll douse 'em."

My gorge rose at the thought of their having to handle those horrible little bodies. But I closed my eyes again and waited, while howls and shouts and sounds like hog-killing time rose from the lake's edge. God knows what the creatures were fed, or how often. They seemed all ribs and swollen bellies. I found it in my soul to regret killing the Unger. According to Lisa, it had not been this way when she lived.

We left the children naked. We had no idea where (or if) they had any clothing. And considering the state of their skins, it was better so. We rigged an awning of a blanket we had brought, so they wouldn't blister. Then we set off across the miles of lake with our cargo of shrieking babies. Behind us we left every house ablaze. There would be nothing there for the Ungers any more. Ever.

The boat flew over the water, its engine throbbing to match my leg. The breeze cooled me a bit, but I knew that I had fever...my bones felt light, and I was dizzy. But at last the dust of white specks we had headed toward became a house with a pier, outbuildings, and a white painted fence. It looked too well kept to have been empty for months.

As we slowed to approach the pier, a middle-aged man waved a shotgun at us from the porch of the house.

"Don't ask," I told Zack. "Leave him two!"

Zack clambered up the short ladder onto the pier, and Elmond handed him a toddler and a three-year-old. He went firmly to the gate that closed off the lawn from the pier and set the children on the overgrown grass. Then he came back and got into the boat. As we sped away, I could see clearly the dumbfounded expression on the man's face. I hoped that he had a wife or a grown daughter.

We found four more occupied houses. One housed an old couple, so we left them only one. A family whose backyard clothesline held many sizes of shirts and pants received three. Anybody with that many children wouldn't have much problem assimilating three more. When we were done, we went home with the two infants.

We came up the river at dusk. The frogs were in full cry. The screech owls were mourning in the bottom-lands, and bobcats were quarreling in the hickory flats. The willows hung straight and still, and wc moved under them, over the bright ripples in which the sunset flared up at us in dying colors.

The babies were quiet, cried out and asleep. Thank God for the goats! We must try to scrounge up several more—they were easy enough for the smaller children to milk, and unlike a cow they wouldn't injure anybody. If we were to keep collecting children it would be necessary. The gentle Nubians were more like pets than livestock.

It was almost dark now. We reached the old river crossing where we were to pull out the boat. There stood Suzi, with all the children except Joseph. One of the babies woke and squealed, and the entire bunch helped to haul out the boat so they could see the new arrivals.

I thought there would be a fight, then and there, to see who got to carry a baby. I sighed. Then Zack picked me up and carried me to the house. I was so utterly exhausted that I forgot to object.

AFTERWORD

So that is the end of the beginning of the story. Now that my leg has healed there is no time to write anymore, though I plan to keep a journal so that I will be able, someday, to give an accurate account of out tribe. When I get too old to stir one foot before the other, maybe I'll have the time to put it into coherent form.

So far we have heard no more from the Ungers, though we know that there are several left in the area. Cheri is alive, we assume, for she was not among those whom Zack helped to bury. As long as she is there, and Ungers are in the woods, they pose some danger, but I think they have been taught a stern lesson and will leave us be, at least for a while. But the time will come when we'll have to take the time to warn those around the lake. There were a lot of boats on the river.

Harley Schmidt came back once. He was much subdued, apologetic, and shocked. He asked us to take in a young man who had managed to make it all the way from Oklahoma City, afoot. He had avoided highways and towns and was all in, needing rest and food. But now he seems to be shaping up very well and I have my eye on him for Suzi.

Carrie Jessup died in her sleep a week ago. Horace, though grief-stricken, is working like six men. He and Grace and Laura have asked La-Tonsha and Lillian to stay with them, and I think the youngsters will go. Little as they are, they feel the need that inspired the invitation.

Sim and Elmond are teaching Jim blacksmithing. They've jury-rigged an anvil, forge, and bellows. As long as we can scrounge iron, we'll be able to work it into useful items. And in my grandmother's girlhood there were iron mines in the northern part of this county. I've marked a map, as nearly as I can determine, with the places she named.

Lucas and Mom Allie have set up housekeeping together. At least as much as can be done now. And Lantana spent so much time nursing Skinny that they decided to comfort each other's old bones. At least, that's what they say. I catch them holding hands when nobody's looking.

Up and down the river we have our crops in, and our fuel and feed stored. Our hatches are battened down, once again, for November is upon us. One short year ago we lived in a world of politics and TV and instant communication. Now we live in a world bounded by the forest and the lake and the river.

We never knew—and likely never will—exactly what triggered the end of things. Neville, our new hand, says that there was no warning of any kind before and no explanation after the blowup. The country he came through was much like this, scantily populated by people who knew nothing. It may be just as well.

Sim is teaching me what he knows of wounds and injuries. With my scrounged medical books and my steady fingers, I just may be able to cope with that hot appendix, if and when. Meanwhile, all work, visit back and forth when we can manage it, and read and read and read.

The world has ended, but we are just beginning.

ABOUT THE AUTHOR

The author of sixty-two books, more than forty of them published commercially, **ARDATH MAYHAR** began her career in the early eighties with science fiction novels from Doubleday and TSR. Atheneum published several of her young adult and children's novels. Changing focus, she wrote westerns as **Frank Cannon** and mountain man novels as **John Killdeer**. Four prehistoric Indian books under her own name came out from Berkley. Historical western ***High Mountain Winter*** was published by Berkley Books under the byline **Frances Hurst**.

Recently she has been working with on-line publishers. ***A Road of Stars*** was her first original novel to appear in a print-on-demand format. Many of her out-of-print titles are now available from e-publishers fictionwise.com and renebooks.com; other OP novels are soon to be reprinted via Wildside Press and Amazon.com.

Now in her seventies, Mayhar was widowed in 1999, after forty-one years of marriage, and has four grown sons. The bookshop she ran with her husband for fifteen years was closed after his death. She now works at home, writing short fiction and nonfiction, and doing book doctoring professionally. Her web pages can be found at:

w2.netdot.com/ardathm/
and
http://ofearna.us/books/Mayhar/books.html

2673051

Made in the USA